AN INTRODUCTION

Having heard his name mentioned, Davis shifted his gaze off J.T. and to the young woman. Tipping his hat, he greeted the lady, then looked back at the man in black.

"Don't I know you, mister? Your face sure seems familiar," asked Davis.

Before J.T. could answer, Josh cut in with a comment.

"I don't think you'd want this fellow knowing you too well, Jed. This is John Thomas Law, the bounty man."

In the blink of an eye the situation around the buggy took a serious turn. On hearing the name, Jed Davis uttered the word, "Damn!" and slapped leather, but before his gun cleared the holster, he heard the hammer go back and found himself staring down the barrel of J.T.'s Colt Peacemaker . . .

DON'T MISS THESE
ALL-ACTION WESTERN SERIES
FROM THE BERKLEY PUBLISHING GROUP

THE GUNSMITH by J. R. Roberts
Clint Adams was a legend among lawmen, outlaws, and ladies.
They called him . . . the Gunsmith.

LONGARM by Tabor Evans
The popular long-running series about Deputy U.S. Marshal
Long—his life, his loves, his fight for justice.

SLOCUM by Jake Logan
Today's longest-running action Western. John Slocum rides
a deadly trail of hot blood and cold steel.

BUSHWHACKERS by B. J. Lanagan
An action-packed series by the creators of Longarm! The
rousing adventures of the most brutal gang of cutthroats ever
assembled—Quantrill's Raiders.

DIAMONDBACK by Guy Brewer
Dex Yancey is Diamondback, a Southern gentleman turned
con man when his brother cheats him out of the family fortune. Ladies love him. Gamblers hate him. But nobody pulls
one over on Dex . . .

WILDGUN by Jack Hanson
The blazing adventures of mountain man Will Barlow—from
the creators of Longarm.

TEXAS TRACKER by Tom Calhoun
Meet J.T. Law: the most relentless and dangerous manhunter
in all Texas. Where sheriffs and posses fail, he's the best
man to bring in the most vicious outlaws—for a price.

TEXAS TRACKER

THE WACO GANG

TOM CALHOUN

JOVE BOOKS, NEW YORK

THE WACO GANG

A Jove Book / published by arrangement with
the author

PRINTING HISTORY
Jove edition / August 2002

Visit our website at
www.penguinputnam.com

ISBN: 0-515-13349-3

A JOVE BOOK®
Jove Books are published by The Berkley Publishing Group,
a division of Penguin Putnam Inc.,
375 Hudson Street, New York, New York 10014.
JOVE and the "J" design
are trademarks belonging to Penguin Putnam Inc.

PRINTED IN THE UNITED STATES OF AMERICA

10 9 8 7 6 5 4 3 2 1

ONE

✡

THE CONDUCTOR CAME through the door dressed in his black coat, crisp-starched white shirt, bowtie and square visor hat. Closing the door behind him, he started down the aisle announcing the next stop on the railroad line.

"Austin comin' up, folks. Austin. Twenty minutes."

John Thomas Law didn't bother to look up as the man passed; his eyes and thoughts were fixed on a handsomely engraved gold watch that he held open in his hand. There was a picture inside. It had been taken in Paris, France, at the same time the watch had been purchased. Opposite the picture the master engraver had written the words J.T. had read over and over countless times for the last ten years: *To John Thomas with all my love, Sara.*

As he read the words his eyes lingered on the picture of a young woman in her late teens. She had long, golden hair that flowed down beyond her shoulders. The eyes were soft, yet penetrating and the face, a thing of beauty. Her name was Sara Jane Woodall, and she wore an ivory brooch on her blouse depicting a willow tree flanked by two doves. The man knew the brooch well. It had belonged to his mother.

Knowing of her son's love for the girl, she had given it to him to give to Sara.

J.T. Law had traveled four hundred miles to see her for the first time after ten long years. The last time he had seen her was before her parents had shipped her off to Paris. She had bought the watch and had the picture made there, then sent it to him as a sign of their love and wrote him faithfully every week. But then had come the Civil War: A war that had pitted brother against brother, fathers against sons and the steadfast southern Law family against the unionist Woodall family. She had remained in Paris throughout the war. Gradually the letters had stopped coming. Somehow the years had slipped away.

J.T. had returned home to a defeated cause and a state that had been ravished by war, corrupt politicians and marauding Comanches. His family had lost everything: their money, the Bar L Ranch, cattle and land. It proved a loss his parents could not bear. His mother died just before John had come home. His father, disillusioned and lost without his mate of thirty-five years, simply gave up and died. There was nothing left besides bitterness and resentment. J.T. had left Texas before Sara returned. Like everything else, when the letters stopped he figured he had lost her as well. For the next few years he traveled from place to place, a lost and often desperate man and not above resorting to crime to make his way.

A former guerrilla fighter and member of the notorious Bloody Bill Anderson Command, he had perfected the art of horsemanship and proved to be a natural when it came to the use of firearms of any kind. At the age of twenty-one, his speed and accuracy with pistol or rifle had earned him the respect of every man in the command, especially two older members who had taken it upon themselves to watch over him during those bloody and violent years.

It was those same two comrades who later saved his bacon during a botched bank robbery in Kansas. The bank had been owned by the same big outfit back east that had literally stolen the Bar L after the war. J.T. hadn't looked at it as a real bank robbery—to him it was more like collecting on an unpaid balance. If there was any robbery done, it had been on the part of the bank. With his saddlebags full of cash, a young J.T. had gotten himself boxed in a canyon by a posse fully intent on sending him to his maker.

Just when all seemed lost, the two old friends from the war came riding straight down that canyon firing Colt .44's with both hands and giving the Rebel yell so loud it could be heard three miles down the canyon walls. Losing four of their comrades, the remainder of the posse had wasted no time getting out of there while the ex–guerilla fighters paused to reload. J.T.'s two saviors that day had been none other than Frank James and Cole Younger.

J.T. had rode with the James-Younger gang for two years. While most spent their ill-gotten gains, J.T. had saved his and when he was ready, bid the group good luck and farewell. No longer broke and destitute, he returned to Texas. The gold watch had traveled with him everywhere he went and the picture was a constant reminder of what could have been had it not been for the war.

In a trick of fate or justice, depending how one looks at such things, J.T. had planned to buy the family ranch back from the bank that held the paper and pay them with their own money. Money he and the James boys had been robbing from their banks all over Kansas and Missouri. Ironically, those same bank owners back east had lost so much money from the robberies that they had to fold, and the ranch was sold at auction. The new owner had split the property up and sold it off in sections until there was no longer a Bar L Ranch, but rather acres and acres of plowed fields and farmhouses.

It seemed that all his efforts had been for nothing. He didn't want any other ranch. He'd tried settling in but after all the years of war and riding with the most famous gang in the country, ranching seemed mighty boring. He began to drink and gamble a lot, until finally he had frittered away all his money. Nearly broke and with no place to call home, J.T. resorted to the only skill he knew—the gun. But he had vowed to Cole and Frank that his outlaw days were over and he had meant it.

It was during a poker game one night that a cowboy had mentioned that he had witnessed a gunfight up in Dodge on his last cattle drive. A fellow named Josh Randall had squared off with two tough hombres in the middle of the street. When the smoke cleared, the town was burying the two outlaws, and Randall was riding out with close to two thousand dollars in his saddlebags—bounty money offered for the two men, dead or alive.

That conversation had stayed with J.T., and the following morning he had walked into the sheriff's office, pulled a bunch of wanted posters off the wall, got himself a partner and set out on a new career. To outlaws, J.T. Law had become one of the most feared gunfighters and bounty hunters in the state of Texas. No less than nineteen men had been sent to their maker looking down the barrel of the bounty man's Colt .45 Peacemaker. Having been an outlaw himself, J.T. knew full well the tension and hardship of constantly being hunted. For that reason he always gave those he was after a choice—give it up or fight it out. Of the twenty-one men he had pursued, only two had submitted to arrest, preferring prison to a pine box and six feet of dirt.

His last job had been a long and hard one. He had tracked down the murderous Baxter Boys after they had gone on a rampage across Texas, killing, robbing and raping. He had looked at the watch and Sara's picture often during that chase and vowed to go and see her when it was over. Somehow in his own mind he had hoped for a respectful and joyous reunion, but that was not to be. After traveling four hundred miles he arrived at his former lover's home only to have the door slammed in his face by a butler who informed him that, "Miss Woodall has no desire to see, nor speak to you, now or at any other time."

Not quite the reception he had envisioned. He had walked away from the house feeling like a complete fool. But then, what could he expect? After all, ten years was a damn long time to get around to making a house call. As he turned to close the gate, he glanced up at one of the second-story windows of her home and saw the corner of the curtains move. She was watching him. He could feel her eyes on him. As he walked away, he couldn't help but think that somehow this was not over between them. If she didn't care, why was she watching him? It was enough for him to hold out hope that someday she would change her mind and at least meet with him. He was a stubborn man. He would be back.

J.T. was about to put his watch away when suddenly the engineer hit the brakes. The passengers were thrown forward as sparks flew from the big wheels and the high-pitched scream of metal against metal carried through the car. J.T.'s head slammed against the seat in front of him. The gold watch flew out of his hand and slid out into the aisle. Women were screaming and men were cussing as they picked themselves up off the floor. They had been thrown around inside the car like rag dolls.

"What the damn hell is goin' on!" shouted a man in the rear of the car.

J.T., momentarily dazed, sat back in his seat and tried to clear his head. Glancing out into the aisle he saw the watch. As he reached down to retrieve it, a boot suddenly came down hard on his hand and a gruff, gravely voice barked, "Leave it be, mister an' get yer ass back in that seat!"

Ignoring the pain to his hand, J.T. looked up into the barrel of a Colt .44 held by a big man with a bandanna covering half his face. Placing the barrel of the gun against J.T.'s forehead, the man slowly cocked the hammer back.

"What? Ya don't hear good, mister? I said put yer ass back in that seat—now!"

J.T. pulled his hand free of the man's boot and slowly sat up, taking note of the cold look he was receiving from the man with the hard brown eyes and an ugly scar across the bridge of his nose. Three more men with their faces covered entered the car as the train chugged to a stop. They were heavily armed and it was clear they meant business. Brown Eyes reached down and picked up the watch, admiring it for a moment. He nodded his approval and muttered from under the mask, "Thanks, friend. I needed a new watch." With that he moved on back to the rear of the passenger car.

There was the roar of a pistol as one of the new arrivals shot a hole in the roof of the car.

"All right, folks! Now that I got yer attention, y'all know what we're here for, so let's get to it. Unlimber them wallets and pokes, ya fellows—an ladies, y'all strip off that jewelry. We'll be takin' that along as well. Anybody looks like they're gonna give us a problem here, they'll get theirself shot on the spot. So get it up, folks. My boys'll be along to collect. Let's go!"

J.T. reached inside his frock coat for his wallet. As he did, his fingers lingered on the grips of the short-barrel Colt .45 he had concealed in a shoulder holster. For a second he calculated the odds. There were three men in front of him and Brown Eyes behind him. Taking down the three in front would require surprise, speed and accuracy. He knew he could handle that. The problem was the man behind him. Could he take the three in front and still make the turn to the rear and get off a shot before Brown Eyes put lead in him?

Influenced by the possible loss of his watch, he convinced himself that it was worth the risk and was about to make his move when his eyes fixed on the frightened face of a young mother across the aisle, clutching a baby in her arms. Looking down the length of the car he counted four more women with children seated between him and the outlaws. He quickly realized this was not the place for a gunfight with four train robbers. There would be plenty of lead flying in a confined space and it was a damn good bet that some of the women and kids could be hit before it was all over. As much as he wanted to take this bunch on and get his watch back, it wasn't worth the life one of these innocent women or children.

Removing his wallet from the inside pocket of his coat, he dropped it into the open grain sack the men were using to collect their ill-gotten gains. Disgusted by the turn of events, J.T. stared out the window. For the first time since the train had been stopped he noticed four mounted outlaws with rifles positioned at various intervals along the length of the train. Looking out the window across the aisle he counted four more masked men that had taken up similar positions on that side. He was impressed. All had rifles and were well mounted. But what really drew his attention was the manner with which the outlaws sat their horses. Ramrod straight, with shoulders back and rifles resting on the thigh, ready for immediate action should it become necessary.

A veteran himself, J.T. recognized a cavalryman when he saw one, and right now he knew he was looking at eight well-trained troopers. Shifting his attention back to the four men inside the train, he began to study their appearance and movements. It was a natural thing for a man in his profession. Once a bounty hunter took up a wanted man's trail he had to learn everything about the man he was after, no matter how small it might seem at the time. J.T. had learned over the years to memorize a description down to the last detail. Hair, eyes, build, any identifying scars, was he left-handed or right-handed, what kind of pistol or rifle did he carry, what color and kind of horse, anything special about the saddle, did it have initials or special design or ornaments. These were all part of the job, and a hunter needs to know what he's doing. More than a few in the profession had ended up swinging from a rope provided by local citizens for killing the wrong man.

He was equally impressed with the group in the train. They had tactically placed themselves at various locations within the car, which would allow for maximum observation while at the same time positioning themselves so that should someone challenge them, as he had considered earlier, they would not hit each other in an exchange of gunfire. This wasn't just another train robbery—it was a train robbery being carried out with perfect military precision.

As the men went about their business, J.T. began to catalog their appearance and movements. They might hold the upper-hand right now, but they were going to be seeing him again, and soon. They could count on that.

The train was suddenly shaken by a violent explosion. J.T. figured that was the express car safe being opened and he was right. The leader of the group looked at his watch and muttered, "Right on time. Hurry up, boys, we gotta be goin'."

J.T. glanced back behind him, searching for sign of Brown

Eyes. He caught a glimpse of him just as the big man went out the back door. Again J.T. felt the temptation to go for his gun. Without the man behind him, he knew he could take the remaining three. But then what? More than likely, his actions would do no more than invite a hailstorm of bullets from the mounted men with the rifles. Common sense prevailed. His watch was gone. He was going to have to accept that for now. He would get it back, but this wasn't the time or place.

"We thank ya kind folks for your patience and cooperation. Now ya stay seated an we'll be on our way. In case ya didn't notice, we got boys on both sides of this train. Anybody goes stickin' his head out, they're libel to get it blowed clean off. Let's go, boys."

J.T. watched the men with loot mount and ride away. Then, with the same precision they had demonstrated during the robbery, the mounted riflemen began to withdraw. One man on each side of the train turned and rode out thirty yards, then turned back toward the train. Raising their rifles and keeping them pointed at the train, they remained in that position while each of their comrades peeled off and rode away. Once they were clear, the two rifleman booted their weapons and withdrew as well. It was a perfect rear-guard withdrawal.

The passenger car was alive with excited chatter as the train began to move again. The young woman across the aisle held her baby close and looking over at J.T. said, "Thank you, sir."

Surprised at her remark, he asked, "For what, ma'am?"

She allowed a slight smile to etch its way across her gentle face.

"I could see that watch meant a lot to you, and you appear to be a man that is accustomed to taking action in situations such as this. I could see it in your eyes—you were ready to fight those men. But you thought of me and my daughter and the other women and children on this train. I'm grateful to you for that, sir."

John T. found himself almost embarrassed. He had never been good at taking compliments, especially from women.

"I am sorry about your watch," she said.

"Oh, that's all right, ma'am. I'll be getting it back one of these days. You can count on that."

Flashing another smile, she replied, "I don't doubt that at all, sir."

The conductor reappeared once again. There was a trace of blood and a nasty-looking bruise along the left side of his forehead. He went about the car trying to restore some sense of calm by asking the passengers to make out a list of the valuables that they had lost so that it could be turned over to the proper authorities when they pulled into Austin. As he started to walk by J.T., the bounty man reached out and grabbed the conductor's arm.

"What about the express car?" he asked.

The conductor stared at the man in black for a moment, clearly trying to put a name to this familiar face. Then it came to him.

"You're J.T. Law, aren't you? The gunfighter and bounty man, right?"

At the conductor's mention of the name, the passengers suddenly fell silent, their eyes directed to the pair. It was a name that most of them had heard or read about in the papers.

"You're him, ain't ya?" asked a man a few seats forward. "The man that tracked down and killed them murderin' Baxter brothers a few months ago."

"Thought I recognized you, Mr. Law," said the conductor. "To answer your question, they killed our express agent and the two guards with him. Got away with pert' near thirty-five thousand dollars. The company will be offering a reward for sure. You going after them Mister Law?"

"They took my gold pocket watch—what'd you think?"

The young conductor grinned from ear to ear as he looked at the staring faces of the passengers.

"Folks, you might not get your valuables back, but with Mister John Thomas Law here going after those boys, you can rest assured you're going to get some justice. I'd say their train robbing days are over—they just don't know it yet."

"Here! Here!" shouted someone as the others began to

cheer and applaud for the man in black whom they now considered their own personal "terrible swift sword of justice." For a second time John T. felt his face go flush from embarrassment. He wanted to strangle the conductor, but politely nodded his thanks to those around him instead.

Thankfully, Austin wasn't that far away. Calm had been restored and everyone was traveling the final few miles in silence or quiet conversation. A few seats back, two young women were eyeing the tall man in black closely—admiring his broad shoulders, his well-groomed black hair and those haunting blue-green eyes that had sent a thrill though them when he had stood earlier and nodded in their direction. They guessed him to be in his mid-thirties and they were right.

The train pulled slowly into the Austin depot. As John T. stood and walked by the two young women that had been admiring him from afar, he touched his fingers to the brim of his hat and smiled. The women blushed and he heard them giggling to each other as he stepped off the train. The depot became a veritable den of excitement as word of the train robbery quickly spread. Passengers couldn't wait to tell friends and family of their harrowing experience. With his bag in hand, J.T. left the depot and headed down the street for the Manor House, one of the finest hotels in Austin. Once he got a room and dropped off his bag he planned to visit his old friend Abe Covington.

TWO

✶

THE HEADQUARTERS FOR the Texas Rangers was located a few blocks from the hotel. As John T. rounded the corner he found the Ranger compound in a state of hurried excitement and a flurry of activity. Standing right in the middle of it all, calmly directing the scene of orderly confusion was Abe Covington. Six foot tall, with broad shoulders and a pair of arms like matching tree trunks. The man with the chestnut hair and Victorian mustache was waving his arms and shouting orders to his charges like an officer in Her Majesty's Cold Stream Guards.

One detachment of Rangers were already mounted and ready to ride. Another was scrambling to get their mounts cinched up and on line. It was obvious his old friend had already got the word about the train robbery. Lighting up a cigar, John T. leaned back against the wall of the Ranger building and watched the show. In a matter of seconds he felt Abe Covington's penetrating brown eyes on him, but only for a fleeting moment.

By the time he had finished his smoke, the dust cleared to reveal two rows of Rangers in a line, sitting in their saddles ramrod straight and awaiting further orders from their commander, Captain Abe Covington. The men were given the details of the robbery, the location and a general description of the men and horses involved. The engineer had said the outlaws had split up and rode off in four different directions after leaving the train. The Rangers were to ride as a group to the robbery site. Once there, they were to spread out and locate the various trails of the outlaws. Once found, the lawmen would disperse in four-man groups to track down and effect an arrest if possible, but should they put up a fight, belly-down over a saddle was equally acceptable.

"Are there any questions, gentlemen?" boomed Covington in his deep baritone voice.

There were none.

"Then get after 'em, boys, an' keep me informed whenever you can."

One of the Rangers yelled out, "Right turn!"

The two lines turned and were now a double column. "Forward—yoo!"

The Rangers disappeared down the street, headed for the depot and the long miles of track beyond. Abe Covington watched them until they were out of sight, then turned to John Thomas Law.

"Understand you were on that train, John T. Didn't believe it at first. They tellin' it right?"

John T. tossed the stub of his cigar to the ground as he replied, "Ya heard right. Why would you find that so hard to believe? Ya know I have been known to ride a train before, Abe."

"I know, J.T. That ain't it. What I found hard to believe, was that with you on it, that train didn't come pullin' into the station with dead men layin' all over the place."

John T. nodded. "Yeah, well, it wasn't because I didn't think about it, that's for damn sure. The sonsabitches stole my gold watch."

Abe motioned for them to go into his office. The Ranger was well aware of the history behind that gold memento.

"Jesus. An you didn't kill a single one of them boys?"

John T. shook his head as the two men walked inside.

"Naw. Too many women and kids in the passenger car.

Some of 'em would've been hurt or killed for sure if there'd been any gunplay. Couldn't chance it."

Abe moved around behind his desk and set down.

"Figured there had to be a good reason for you to hold back. Them folks don't know how lucky they were."

J.T. thought of the young mother with the baby. "One of 'em does."

Abe was pulling a bottle of whiskey out of the top drawer of the desk. Looking up, he asked, "What was that, John T.?"

"Nothin', Abe. You still drinkin' that god-awful snakebite medicine you call whiskey?"

Covington smiled. "Sure am. Know ya hate the stuff, but ya want one, right?"

"Guess it'll have to do till I can find some real drinkin' whiskey."

Abe laughed as he poured two glasses to the brim and passed one over to J.T. Sitting back in his chair, Abe took a hefty shot of the whiskey then asked, "J.T., any idea on who them boys might be that pulled that train job?"

John T. made a face as he forced down half of his glass of whiskey. God, the stuff was terrible, but Abe had been drinking it for years and it hadn't killed him yet.

"No idea, Abe. But I'll tell you one thing—most, if not all them boys, were ex-cavalrymen."

This statement quickly got the Ranger's attention. Leaning forward in his chair, he asked, "How you figure that, John T.?"

"By the way they operated, for one thing. Look at the spot they picked to stop the train. Open prairie all around so their lookouts could see anybody comin' for miles. They worked in teams: one group in the train, one for the express car and a third group, mounted flankers on both sides of the train with Winchesters to make sure nobody got off. The kicker was the way the flankers sat their horses—pure cavalry, if I ever saw it."

J.T. paused a moment to finish off his whiskey.

"No sir, Abe. Some things a fellow don't forget. A sergeant kickin' your butt and screamin' in your face everyday about how to sit a horse in a military fashion—now that's something that stays with a man for life."

"Well I'll be damned," exclaimed Abe, who leaned forward and began sifting through the stack of papers on his desk.

"Now where are those telegrams I got yesterday? Ah, here we are. Listen to this. It's from the sheriff of Cordova up in McLennan County.

CORDOVA BANK ROBBED THIS MORNING. STOP. EIGHT OUTLAWS INVOLVED. STOP. TWO BANK EMPLOYEES, TWO CITIZENS KILLED. STOP. POSSE AMBUSHED BY UNKNOWN NUMBER OF MEN WHILE IN PURSUIT LESS THAN TWO MILES FROM TOWN. STOP. THREE POSSE KILLED, ONE WOUNDED. LOSS ESTIMATED AT $15,000 DOLLARS. STOP.
          CHARLIE RICHARDS, MARSHALL, CORDOVA

Abe set that one aside then began reading another one. "I got this one this morning. It's from the sheriff in McLennan County."

TRAIN TO WACO FROM AUSTIN ROBBED THIS A.M. STOP. 12–15 MEN BELIEVED INVOLVED. STOP. NO BODY HURT. STOP. EXPRESS CAR SAFE DYNAMITED. STOP. $20,000 DOLLARS STOLEN. STOP. POSSE FOUND TRACKS. OUTLAWS DISPERSED IN FOUR DIRECTIONS. STOP. WILL TRY TO FOLLOW. STOP.
          JOE WRIGHT, SHERIFF, MCLENNAN COUNTY

"What'd ya think of that, J.T.?" asked Covington.

John T. stood and walked to the huge map of Texas that hung on the wall beside Abe's desk. He studied it for a minute before he answered.

"Well, it couldn't be the same bunch that hit us. They couldn't have covered that much ground that fast even if they'd been using relay horses. Nope. You're dealin' with two groups of train robbers here, Abe."

"Whaddya' make of the bank robbery in Cordova?"

John T. poured himself another drink. "I'd say you got yourself a problem, ol' friend. You got three holdups in the last twenty-four hours. I can't prove it, mind you—but I'd be willing to bet good money that all three are somehow connected."

Covington stared at the map. "So you're sayin' it's all part of the same gang?"

"Like I said, it's just a guess, mind you. But yeah, I am. I'll tell you why. If you wire that Sheriff Wright in Waco and ask for more details about the robbery, I'll bet it'll pretty well fit with what I saw happen on my train this afternoon."

J.T. saw the confused look on the Ranger's face as Abe asked, "An' just how'd you figure that?"

"Couple of reasons. One, the size of the gang used at the Waco robbery. That's about how many worked the Austin train. Two, like this one here, they split up and rode off in all directions and finally, there's the bank at Cordova."

Abe looked totally confused now. Sitting down, he took a long, hard swig straight from the bottle before asking, "Yer givin' me a damn headache here. I guess ya know that. Now, you wanta explain that one?"

John Thomas gave a halfhearted laugh. "Think about it for minute, Abe. Eight men ride into a town to rob a bank. More than likely four went inside while the other four watched the street. They come out, there's some shootin' and they ride out. Few minutes later a posse hightails it after 'em only to get ambushed less than two miles from town by another group that's been layin' for a posse they knew would be giving chase. Don't you get it, Abe? That posse was ambushed by a rear-guard element that had moved into position before them boys ever set foot in that bank. What you had at Cordova was a well-executed plan carried out with the same military precision as the two train robberies. That's why I think they're all somehow connected."

Abe took another swig from the bottle before he replied, "Yer right, J.T. Looks like we got a real problem on our hands. A damn sizeable problem at that if your idea holds water. Hellfire, we could be dealin' with a bunch that has maybe forty or fifty guns ridin' for 'em."

J.T. lit up a cigar and sat back in his chair. "That's right, Abe. But your real problem is the man that put this bunch together. That man knows his business. He not only picked men that can ride and shoot, but ex-military men that are well-disciplined and accustomed to taking orders. What he's done is put together a pretty damn formidable army of his own."

Abe frowned. "Yeah, and it's payin' off damn well for him, too. Thirty-five thousand dollars from the Austin train, another twenty thousand outside Waco and fifteen thousand dollars from the bank in Cordova. Hell, that's seventy thousand dollars in twenty-four hours!"

The total dollar amount stunned the lawman as he heard himself repeat it for a second time, and then shook his head. "Seventy thousand dollars—god. The governor's gonna be screamin' for someone's ass if we don't get a handle on this, an' damn quick."

John Thomas stood and started for the door. "Well, Abe. Appears you're gonna be plenty busy for awhile so I'll get out of your way. Thanks for the whiskey—I think. See you later."

Covington jumped up from his chair and hurried around from behind his desk.

"Now wait a minute, John T. I'm gonna need some help corralin' this bunch. Ya seem to have 'em figured out pretty good. What'd ya say? Can ya help us out here? Less I miss my guess, the bank and the railroad will be puttin' up a damn sizeable reward for these boys before it's over."

J.T. paused at the door. Abe was right. There was money to be made, especially from the railroad, an outfit that had deep pockets and didn't mind digging into them. They'd offer reward money, dead or alive—preferably dead.

Abe saw that he had the bounty man's attention.

"Less of course ya wanta let me swear ya in and hang one of these here Ranger badges on that shirt."

John Thomas gave a half grin and shook his head.

"Abe, you know better than that. All that badge does is tangle a fellow up in the legal end of this business. Warrants, lawyers and judges that take the constitution too damn seri-

ous when it comes to dealing with murderers, rapist and killers. They're so damn busy worrying about rights that they
forget the people who died. No thanks. I don't need no
badge." Slapping his hand against the Colt Peacemaker on
his hip, J.T. continued, "This is all the warrant, judge and
jury I need."

Abe was about to argue some of the finer points of the
law, when Hogie Matthews, who ran the telegraph office,
came into the office.

"Cap'n, got a wire here for ya from the sheriff in Waco,"
said the short, stocky-built man who was breathing hard from
his hurried pace.

Abe read the telegram then passed it over to John Thomas
as he said, "Okay, Hogie. I'll be by your place in a little
while with a reply. Thanks."

"No problem, Cap'n. Whenever yer ready."

As the little man left, J.T. read the message. A gang of
ten to fifteen rustlers had killed four drovers and stolen a
herd of close to one thousand cattle from the Circle H—one
of the largest ranches south of Waco. It was the third such
raid in the area in a month. The telegram made it clear that
the ranchers wanted help from the Rangers.

Abe rubbed his head as he said, "Damnit, that's all I need
right now, another case of rustlin' comin' outta that county.
That's the third time they hit the ranchers up there this
month. They swoop down, shoot up the drovers and hightail
it with the cattle. 'Fore anybody knows what's goin' on,
they're halfway to Mexico. Sure didn't need that kinda news
today." Abe paused a moment, then looking at J.T. asked,
"Ya don't think this business could somehow be linked to
the same bunch, do ya?"

J.T. walked back over to the map. Three out of four of
the incidents of the last twenty-four hours had occurred in
McLennan County and seemed to center around Waco. If a
fellow was going to look into this business, Waco would be
the place to start. Pondering Abe's question, J.T. gave Abe
an answer.

"I don't know, Abe. Guess it could be part of the same

outfit. Fellow'd have to ride up there to check it out, I suppose. You know this Sheriff Wright?"

"Met him a couple of times. Why ya askin'?"

J.T. dropped the telegram on to the pile that had began to accumulate on the Ranger's desk.

"Just seems to me there's a lot of activity goin' on up in that part of the country. You'd think with large groups of outlaws and rustlers ridin' north, south and west of Waco, the law could catch at least one or two of them fellows. But you got two telegrams here and no mention of a single one captured, or even killed, for that matter. Don't you find that kind of strange? Either that bunch is awful damn good at what they do, or your lawman up there needs to find another line of work."

"Now wait a minute here, John T.—just what are ya sayin'?"

"Not sayin' anything, Abe. Just thinkin' out loud, that's all."

J.T. walked across the room and opened the door. Looking back at the Ranger captain, he smiled.

"I'm at the Manor House. Gonna get me a hot bath an' a little sleep. Why don't you join me for dinner tonight. I'll buy you a steak and some real whiskey for a change instead of that kerosene you drink."

Abe grinned for the first time that afternoon. "Yer on. What time?"

"Make it about seven. See you later, Abe."

The Ranger stood in the doorway watching the big man walk down the street. He'd known John Thomas Law for a few years now and one thing he'd discovered about the manhunter and gunfighter, he was a lot sharper that people gave him credit for. The man was smart, observant and deadly— all necessary requirements for those that engaged in the bounty hunting profession. Few in Texas would deny that J.T. Law was the best in the business. No less than 19 men had met their maker in fair and legal face-to-face confrontations with the bounty man. But unlike many in the business who thought nothing of back-shooting a wanted man, J.T. always gave his man the option of surrendering to the law or trying his luck with the iron on his hip. It was a virtue that had earned the ex-Rebel the respect of not only a number of lawmen, but many of the wanted men that roamed Texas as well.

Closing the door, Abe went back to the map on the wall. J.T. was right. Whoever was running this outfit had put together his own private army and for now were having it all their way. Seventy thousand dollars and one thousand head of prime cattle was a damn profitable week, no doubt about it. They didn't know it yet, but they'd made one big mistake today—they had stolen John Thomas Law's gold watch.

THREE

✦

ONE HUNDRED YARDS out from what was once a deserted ranch house located just west of the Brazos River, and partially hidden among the mountain cedars and oaks, twelve wary and dust-covered riders pulled rein and brought their tired horses to a halt. It was just coming on sunset and the light was fading fast.

A big, heavyset man with a beard walked his horse a few feet forward of the group. Fishing around in his vest pocket, he removed a match and brought it to life with his thumbnail. Holding the flame out in front of him with one hand, he placed his other hand in front of the flame, slowly raised it, then lowered it again. He performed this ritual three times, then blew the flame out and waited.

The only sound in the fading light was that made by the leather of a well-worn saddle creaking as the big man shifted his sore butt from one side to the other as he stared out across the one hundred yards of flat open ground before him. As the seconds stretched into minutes, the big man began to get nervous. One of his hands slowly made its way to the grips of the Colt .44 in his holster. He was about to turn his horse back, and lead his men off into the night when suddenly, he saw it: a flare of light across the plain. Bright at first, it then disappeared for a second then reappeared again. It did this twice, then as abruptly as it had come to life, the light went out for good. Turning in his saddle, Deke Toban spoke out in a loud, gravelly tone.

"That's the signal, boys. Let's go."

The men followed their leader out across the flatland at a leisurely pace until they encountered the sentries on the outer perimeter.

"Dixie!" came a clear and threatening challenge from the darkness.

"Steven fuckin' Foster!" came the bellowed reply from the big man in front.

"Deke! That you?"

"Hell, yes it is, Charlie. Who else you expectin' tonight—Jeff Davis?"

The sentry, called Charlie, stepped out of the darkness from behind a tree and walked out to greet them. He put a hand on the neck of Deke's horse.

"You boys made good time. The cap'n wasn't expectin' ya for a couple more hours."

There was weariness in Toban's voice as he asked, "The rest of the boys all back in?"

"Yeah," replied Charlie. "All except for Lieutenant Tom. Him and Choctaw Jones's crew are drivin' a herd down to old Mexico."

There was a clear hint of surprise in Deke's voice. "Herd? What herd?"

Charlie gave a short laugh. "Oh, yeah. I forgot. You and the boys was already gone when the cap'n come up with that one. We hit the Circle H this mornin'. Got away with close to a thousand head."

"Goddamnit, Charlie!" shouted Deke, suddenly in a rage. "That's Tom Harrison's outfit. The man was a damn brigadier general for the Confederacy. We wasn't supposed to be bothering him none. I told the cap'n that right up front. The man's a Southern hero. It don't set well with me and it damn sure won't set well with the other Southern boys neither, I'll tell ya that right now."

Charlie quickly took a couple of steps back as he replied, "Don't be yellin' at me, Deke. I'm just a private in this outfit. You an' the cap'n's the ones that run the show. The cap'n's up at the main house right now. Ya got a problem, ya go on up there an' tell him if in ya got a mind to."

Deke spurred his horse forward as he grumbled, "That just what I'm gonna do."

Charlie sleeved the dust raised by the passing riders from his face. Boy, he sure would like to be up around that house to listen in when Deke went after the cap'n. But that'd be like committin' suicide. By the cap'n's rules, leaving your post was a court-martial offense punishable by a firing squad.

True, this wasn't no real army like in the war, but a fellow would be hard-pressed to convince the men who rode for this outfit of that fact. Just two weeks earlier, down along the border, a crew was driving stolen cattle to Mexico. Two sentries had gone to sleep at their post and allowed a troop of Federals to ride right into the camp. In the gun battle that had followed, three of the crew were killed and two badly wounded before they managed to drive the Mexican troops off. The cap'n held court when they got back. He found the two sentries guilty and had them shot dead ten minutes later.

Every since then, whenever Charlie had sentry duty he made himself a necklace of prickly pear thorns and wore it around his neck. If he started to nod off, his head would drop and the thorns would stick the hell out of him. Painful maybe, but it sure did the trick at keepin' a fellow awake. Besides, a little prick in the neck was a damn sight better than rifle slug in the chest. No, maybe it wasn't no real army, but don't tell the cap'n that.

Arriving at the corral located just to the right, and below the main house, Deke stepped down from his horse and tossed the reins to Frank Boyd, his second-in-command.

"Take care of my horse, Frank. I'm goin' to see that bastard right now."

Pulling the saddlebags filled with the plunder from the Austin train robbery, Big Deke slung them over his broad shoulders and stomped off for the house. Boyd watched his ex-Reb commander take the steps two at a time and disappear inside the house. He wouldn't be surprised to hear gunfire coming from there anytime in the next five minutes. Big Deke Toban was a quick-tempered sonofabitch who was hard as nails and a real handful when he was riled and on the prod. The captain was going to have to talk fast to smooth his feathers if he wanted to avoid any gunplay.

Pulling his newly acquired gold watch from his vest pocket, Boyd flipped it open to check the time. One of the men saw the watch and asked. "Hey, Frank. Ya wanta sell that watch? I'll give ya one hundred dollars hard money for it right now."

Boyd laughed and shook his head.

"Hell, son. The picture inside here's worth mor'n that."

The younger outlaw stepped closer and looked at the picture.

"Well, yer sure right about that, Frank. That's a damn fine-lookin' woman, all right. Bet the fellow ya took that from is mad as hell 'bout now."

Frank nodded his agreement. "Yeah, he wasn't none to happy about it, that's for sure."

As the boy walked away, Frank tilted the watch to the side, and saw there was some writing on the inside. He tried to read it by moonlit, but all he could make out was a name—"John Thomas." The name didn't mean anything to him. Clicking it shut, he shoved it back in his pocket. Glancing up at the house, Frank Boyd uttered, "That damn silver-tongued Yankee captain must have calmed Deke down."

If there hadn't been any shootin' by now, there wouldn't be any. Saddle-wary and bone tired, Frank took his long lanky body toward the bunkhouse and some much-needed sleep.

One of the guards stationed on the porch had seen Toban and his crew arrive and informed the captain. The captain in turn had moved two of his men into the room and placed them on each side of the door. Sitting behind his desk he then removed a Colt .44 from the drawer, cocked the hammer back and placed the gun within easy reach. Deke Toban had proven invaluable putting the outfit together. He was a partner and a friend. But Jack Corbin was nobody's fool. Even after all these years, Big Deke was a sentimentalist when it came to anything dealing with the Confederacy. No doubt he'd already heard about the raid on the Circle H before he reached the corrals.

To Deke, former Confederate General Thomas Harrison was every bit a hero as Robert E. Lee. To steal anything, let alone a thousand head of cattle from the man would be like committing sacrilege against the Holy Church itself. That's how Deke would see it anyway. That was why Corbin had purposely waited until the big man had left before issuing the order for the raid on the Circle H. He knew Deke wouldn't have gone along with it, but business was business. Deke was going to have to understand that.

Texas had been struggling to recover from the effects of the Civil War; now, almost eleven years later, they finally had things on the upswing, thanks to longhorn cattle, a growing populace and plenty of land. There was a lot of money to be made in a growing state like Texas. But it took money to make money—a lot of money.

Money not only bought land, it bought power as well. If handled right, those two things combined could put a man in the governor's chair. That was Jack Corbin's ultimate goal. But to obtain such lofty aspirations would require total commitment and whatever tactics necessary, no matter how ruthless. They couldn't afford to play favorites. Corbin understood that. He had set himself on a path with a clear goal. A goal that for some reason he could not get Deke to fully understand or appreciate.

Any minute now, the former Rebel cavalry officer was going to come through the door snorting like some out-of-control bull in a china shop, screaming that Corbin had somehow violated the sanctity of the Rebel code by stealing cattle from one of the biggest ranches in Texas. That was a certainty. The only question concerning Jack Corbin was just how upset his partner would be when he came through that door. It was that unknown factor that necessitated the guards in the room and gun on the desk. A little drastic perhaps, but Corbin had seen Deke Toban shoot a man dead in Corpus Christi for defaming the name of ex–Confederate President

Jeff Davis. Jack Corbin had stolen a one thousand head of cattle from a Southern hero—there was no telling what Deke would do.

Deke came at full stride bringing his huge frame to a halt squarely in the middle of the room. Jerking the saddlebags from his shoulder, he tossed them to the floor a few feet in front of Corbin's desk, then moved his right hand back to his side, inches from the grip of his Colt .44.

"There's your money from the Austin job—Cap'n! I say 'yer's' because it seems ya've decided to take over this bunch."

Corbin didn't bat an eye. Remaining perfectly still, he answered, "Now why would you say a thing like that, Deke? We're partners. You know that."

A smirk came over Deke's face as he stared hard at the captain. As usual, the man didn't have a hair out of place. The thick head of brown hair was neatly combed and he was dressed to the nines, as was his fashion. Corbin never flinched as he locked his dark brown eyes with those of Deke Toban waiting for an answer.

"Yeah, ya keep tellin' me we're partners, but seems to me yer the one makin' all the decisions, Corbin. Guess I'm supposed to be a silent partner, is that it? We talk and do all the planin' together, then ya ignore anything I say, an' do whatever the hell ya want. That how it works, Corbin? That yer damn Yankee idea of a partner?"

Corbin saw Deke's hand move closer to the .44 on his hip. If the big man pulled that gun his guards were going to shoot him dead. That would shatter a lot more than a partnership: it would split the outfit that had taken Corbin more than a year to put together. Most of the men were ex–Red soldiers. The ramifications of Deke Toban being killed by the captain's Yankee guards was certain to set off a string of retribution that would destroy everything he had been working for. Even if he himself were fortunate enough to survive the aftermath, those left standing would fade away, and with them any hope that the aristocrat captain from Massachusetts had of achieving his goal to run the State of Texas. A highly educated man who was a fast thinker and possessed the gift for gab, Corbin tried to stall while he searched for some kind of answer that would satisfy Toban and lower this dangerous situation down a notch or two.

"This about the Circle H raid, Deke?"

Toban glanced at the guards to the left and right of the door. Corbin wasn't taking any chances. Both men were as loyal to the Yankee captain as the sun to the morning sky.

"Ya know damn well it is, Jack. I thought we had an understandin'. Nobody was to bother the Circle H. Now that seems pretty damn clear to me. Ya wanta tell me what part of that deal ya didn't understand?"

Corbin sat with his fingers interlocked and his hands resting in the center of the desk. True to form, in the short time it had taken Toban to make his statement, Corbin had formulated the perfect answer.

Unlacing his fingers, Corbin raised a hand. "Okay, Deke. Now if you'll just calm down I'll explain."

A frown crossed Deke's face. His hand still remained poised near his gun.

"This better be good, Jack."

Corbin knew the big man was right. He was only going to get one chance to sell his explanation or there was going to be lead flying.

"How many ranches have we hit in the last two months, Deke?"

Toban thought for moment then answered, "Five all together. Three last month and two this month—three if ya count the H., which wasn't supposed to be in the deal."

Suddenly a smile broke across the captain's ruggedly handsome features.

"Exactly, Deke. Think about that for a minute. We hit two spreads to the south, one north, one east and one west of the Circle H. Five outfits all around the H lose cattle, but Tom Harrison don't even have one wander off. Now if you were one of those five wouldn't you start thinking that was kind of queer? Here's the biggest ranch around and they haven't lost a single cow. Wouldn't that seem pretty damn suspicious to you, Deke?"

The room was completely silent for a moment as Toban

considered the question. The tension in the room was so thick Corbin could almost feel the hair on the back of his hand starting to rise. The guards near the door knew exactly what was going on and they were ready. If Toban pulled iron they were going to drop him where he stood.

Deke mulled it over in his head for a minute. What Corbin said made sense. He hadn't thought of that. The only thing worse than stealing the general's cattle was the thought of his neighbors thinking that this honorable man was somehow associated with a band of killers and cattle thieves.

Deke relaxed his gun hand and let it drop to his side.

"Reckon yer right, Jack. Hadn't thought of it that way. Guess it would look pretty damn bad at that. So what yer sayin' is that we done the general a favor by rustlin' his cows. That right?"

The tension in the room had backed off considerably by the dropping of Deke's hand. Corbin had him under control now and he knew it.

"Exactly, Deke," said Corbin, the smile still on his face. "But don't feel bad, partner. I hadn't even thought of it either till I started looking at the map. Then it came to me. I was going to discuss it with you, but you and your outfit had already pulled out for Austin. Knowing how much store you put in the general's reputation, I figured you would have went along if you'd been here. So I ordered the raid. Glad to see I was right."

Frank Boyd had been right. Jack Corbin was every bit the silver-tongued devil he had said he was. In one statement he had not only justified his actions against the Circle H, but had done it in such a way as to not make Deke feel like a fool.

Corbin continued, "Deke, I'll make you a promise. Once we got power in Texas, we'll make it up to general for what we had to do. You got my word on that."

Deke nodded. "That'd be the proper thing to do all right, Jack."

Corbin came from behind his desk and placed his hand on his partner's dust-covered shoulder.

"You look plum wore out, Deke. Why don't you go get

some sleep? We can talk some more tomorrow."

That was one thing the Yankee had right. Deke was bone weary and saddle worn. Silently he nodded in agreement. Turning on his heel Deke walked out onto the front porch. There were three bedrooms in the main house, but Deke Toban preferred to bunk with his men. That was just the kind of man he was. He never placed himself on a higher level than his men. He felt that helped build a stronger sense of camaraderie and trust.

Jack Corbin, on the other hand, saw it as a sign of weakness. Leadership deserved its rewards. He saw better food and better living conditions as symbols of authority that the men under his command could understand. A leader couldn't afford to be just one of the boys. He had always felt that had been Robert E. Lee's only weakness—weakness that eventually cost the South the war.

Standing out on the porch, Corbin lit a cigar as he watched his partner walk down the slope toward the bunkhouses. Weakness was something that Corbin would not tolerate in his organization. He couldn't. The stakes were too high. But there was a time and a place for everything. For now there was little he could do to rectify the situation. More than half of his raider force were made up of ex–Confederate troopers who considered Toban nothing less than another Stonewall Jackson. He needed them all right now. They were key to his plans, but over time, as things progressed and he drew closer to his goal he planned to rid himself of Toban and his men and replace them with his own. Men he felt he could trust not to question his decisions and who didn't have this unwavering sense of honor and dedication to a lifestyle and cause that were lost so long ago. It was just a matter of time.

Walking back into the house, he picked up the saddlebags from in front of the desk and moved to a small room in the back of the house. Removing a chain from his neck that held two keys, Corbin used one to remove a lock from the door and went inside. A large iron chest sat on a table in the center of the room. Using the second key, he removed the heavy padlock from the box and opened it. Dumping the contents of the bags on the table, he began placing the money neatly into the box next to the bags of gold, silver and other currency that took up half the box. Corbin estimated that he had over $150,000 dollars so far. That was a lot of money, but not nearly enough for what he had in mind. Power never did come cheap.

Locking the box and the door to the room, Corbin returned to his desk and studied the map of Texas that lay before him. The former Yankee cavalry officer had broken down the counties ranging from Waco to Austin into various grids, highlighting the ranches located in those areas. Banks and trains were the quickest source of immediate cash, but they also constituted the bigger risk. When you stole from a bank, you stole money from the pockets of every member of that town and irate citizens made for determined posses. The same was true of the powerful railroads who had enough wealth and influence in the right place to get the United States Army involved if necessary to protect their interest.

No, Jack Corbin wasn't going to make a habit of robbing banks and trains. Rustling might not be as easy, or as immediately profitable, but it was a hell of a lot safer. The only people that would kick and scream over that were the ranchers, and Corbin's crew could deal with them. A lawman would have a hard time convincing the people of a town to risk getting shot or killed to chase down outlaws who had stolen something that they themselves had absolutely no financial investment or interest in. The same was true of the railroads. They were paid to haul the cattle; getting them to the railhead was the ranchers' problem, not theirs. So far Corbin's hard-riding, straight-shooting army had knocked enough cowboys out of their saddles to discourage any serious attempts at prolonged pursuit by ranchers or posses.

For now, everything was going Corbin's way. He had done pretty well for himself, but it hadn't always been that way. Coming from a somewhat well-to-do Massachusetts family with ties to New England politics, he had been commissioned as a twenty-eight year-old captain at the beginning of the Civil War. An avid horseman, Corbin had quickly impressed his superiors not only with his horsemanship, but his organizational skills and unique understanding of military tactics. It was this ability that had led to him being assigned to a Michigan cavalry unit commanded by the boy hero George Armstrong Custer, a man Corbin found far too flamboyant, even for his taste.

Present at a number of major campaigns, Corbin continuously distinguished himself in battle after battle. Soon, word began to spread of his courage and daring. But in Custer's command there was only room for one hero and the boy general made sure to keep Captain Jack Corbin in the background whenever the newspaper men came around. Like so many others of that war who had gained a certain degree of fame, Corbin was all but forgotten at war's end. He became just another civilian, while his commander, Custer, went on to national prominence as a supposed great Indian fighter.

Returning home, he found his family had lost everything through bad investments and his father's addiction to gambling. There was nothing left. Filled with anger and resentment, he headed west to find his fortune. What followed was a string of menial jobs that barely served to keep body and soul together. He quickly discovered that the stories and flyers about riches and untold wealth that awaited the adventurer in the west were just that, stories. Outright lies was a better term for it.

After living hand-to-mouth for nearly three long years, the former officer and northern gentleman had had enough of the pauper's life. He soon fell in with a group of men of questionable character and before long found himself a willing participant in an Arizona bank robbery.

The entire job was poorly planned and executed and was doomed to failure from the very start. Corbin had pointed out a number of flaws in the plan, but he was the new man in the outfit and his opinions meant little to the leaders. Against his better judgment, Corbin went along on the robbery. It was a decision that had cost him seven years in the Arizona hellhole prison at Yuma. Wounded and captured, Corbin managed to protect the family name by convincing the law and the court that his real name was Joe Bascome, from Arkansas. It was under that alias that he served his seven years, being released for good behavior in the spring of 1875.

While in prison, Jack began to formulate his plan for Texas. He had learned a number of valuable lessons from the failed robbery. Chief among those: that you didn't work with amateurs. Newspaper stories of the escapades of the James-Younger gang served as an inspiration whenever he would start feeling low. They were living proof that a well-organized, well-armed and highly disciplined force with the right kind of planning and leadership could operate anywhere in the country with a high degree of success. Within a week of his release, Jack Corbin had set his plan into motion.

Four months later he had gathered a force of nearly fifty men, all former veterans of the war, both north and south, and all down on their luck. Chief among them, Deke Toban, who, in a less organized manner, had come up with the same idea of using experienced veterans, but didn't know exactly how to go about putting it all together. Corbin had convinced the man that by joining forces and sharing the leadership, they could all get rich beyond their wildest dreams. Toban liked the sound of that, but what had impressed him most was Corbin's ability to plan and organize. Everything from men, horses, ammunition, food and routes of travel, to establishing an intelligence network. They had paid eyes and ears in practically every town from Dallas to Laredo. Included on that payroll were lawmen, judges and even a few politicians.

The Corbin-Toban gang worked a corridor that was seventy-five miles wide and extended from Dallas to the Mexican border in Laredo. Nothing went on in that established corridor that Jack Corbin didn't know about. From the movement of posses or military troops, to cattle drives and gold shipments by rail or stage. All told it had taken over a year to get everything into place and operational.

Perhaps the most ingenious part of the operation was the establishment of the CT Ranch: a vast one-hundred-thousand-acre spread located thirty miles north of San Antonio. From all outward appearances it was a working cattle ranch with a pretty good size crew. Ironically, Corbin and Toban had purchased the ranch and vast acreage early on with money they had made by stealing Mexican cattle and selling them in Texas.

The CT Ranch served as a way station for stolen cattle being driven south of the border where they were sold to rich Mexican ranchers who cared little about brands or proof of ownership. The Circle H cattle would eventually end up at the CT, where they would be rested for a few days before the final push to the border. Of the one thousand head that had been stolen, three hundred would be cut out and the brands changed, making them part of the ever growing CT herd. Corbin had thought of everything. If he was going to become involved in Texas politics there were sure to be a lot of questions asked about who he was and where he came from. The establishment of the CT and its vast holdings would satisfy the majority of those questions.

It was an elaborate plan that had been formulated in a prison cell eight years ago. A plan that many, had they known about it, would have said was impossible. But who was to say what was impossible? Look at Custer. While thousands revered the golden-haired boy general, Corbin had found him to be an obnoxious, self-centered ass whose arrogance and need for attention and glory would one day place him in situation he couldn't get out of. And that situation had finally come only a few months ago in the Black Hills. Custer's arrogance had led to the death of the hero and his entire command at the hands of the powerful Sioux Nation.

And then of course there was Grant. The supposed savior of the Union who had spent most of the war with a whiskey bottle in his hand. Hell, the man was a goddamn drunk who was now president of the United States, with an administration that was riddled with more graft and corruption than any in past history. So who was to say Jack Corbin couldn't become the governor of Texas? The way he had it figured, he was only a year away from tossing his hat into the ring. Custer and Grant could have their glory and notoriety; he didn't care anymore. He would soon have the money and the power he'd always wanted and that was all that mattered. Calling one of his guards in, he told the man to inform the men they were moving out tonight, heading back to the CT Ranch. This abandoned way station had served its purpose. It was now time to go home.

FOUR

✡

J.T. FELT LIKE a new man. He'd had a good long soak in a steaming hot tub and a sound sleep between crisp, clean sheets on one of the most comfortable mattresses made. It might cost thirty dollars a day for a room at the Manor House, but as far as he was concerned, it was worth every penny.

Slipping on his pants and a freshly laundered white shirt, J.T. put on his vest with the pearl buttons, then the shoulder holster with the short-barreled Colt.45. Next came the highly polished boots he'd bought on his trip to Dallas. They were a little tight, but he'd have them broken in soon enough. Finally came his favorite short-length black frock coat that had been dusted and cleaned. Looking at himself in the mirror, he figured he was still a fairly good-looking man. The face was starting to show a few wrinkles around the eyes and the hair was receding a bit in the front, but considering how he'd lived his life, he didn't look too damn bad for a thirty-six-year-old man.

Abe was supposed to meet him in the restaurant at seven. Reaching into his vest his relaxed mood suddenly changed as he felt the empty pocket where he normally kept his gold watch. It was a stark reminder of the task that lay ahead. But that wouldn't begin until tomorrow. For now, all he could do was put the matter aside, relax and enjoy a fine dinner with an old friend.

As he went down the stairs to the lobby, the desk clerk informed him that Captain Covington was waiting for him in the bar. J.T. nodded his thanks to man and crossed the lobby, pausing long enough to glance into the restaurant. The place was full of people, with others waiting near the double doors for a table to open up. That was probably why Abe was in the bar. He wasn't really much on crowded restaurants.

J.T. found the Ranger sitting at a corner table, a bottle of the hotel's finest whiskey occupied the center. As J.T. approached the table, Abe looked up.

"Well, well. Ain't we all gussied up. We got the Queen of England joinin' us or do ya dress that way whenever ya put on the feed bag?"

J.T. gave a laugh as he sat down and poured himself a drink.

"No, Abe. I did it all just for you. A Ranger's judged by the company he keeps. Didn't you know that?"

The Ranger grinned. "Didn't know that. Guess bein' here with you means my reputation just went all to hell then."

The aged whiskey went down smooth as J.T. said, "Well, some of my good manners must be rubbin' off on you, Abe. You're learnin' what good whiskey tastes like."

"Not really. I just ask the man what was the most expensive whiskey they had and he plopped that down in front of me. Said it was the best in the house, but damn expensive. Told him that'd be fine—you was buyin'."

Both men laughed and poured another round of drinks. They were about to start discussing the robberies and J.T.'s theory when J.T. noticed a young man about twelve or thirteen come into the outer lobby with a huge stack of newspapers stuck under his arm. Rising one of the papers high above his head and waving it around, he began yelling, "Extra! Extra! James Gang wiped out in Minnesota! Three killed. Youngers captured!"

Within seconds the boy was surrounded by a mob of people all wanting a paper. J.T. sat momentarily stunned by the news. He lowered his glass onto the table and seemed to be staring off into space.

"You all right, John T.?" asked Abe.

J.T. didn't hear a word the man said. Jumping to his feet, he hurried out into the lobby for a paper. Reading as he walked, he made his way back to the table and sat down. Abe saw the intensity in his friend's face as he read the story.

He and John Thomas Law hadn't talked much about the war, and when they did, it was Abe who had done all the talking. He was sure J.T. had fought somewhere, but the man never mentioned it, and Abe hadn't pushed it, But some of the Rangers that had witnessed the bounty man's riding and shooting abilities were convinced that he had been a cavalryman during the war, and not just regular cavalry at that. There was only one place the man could have learned his unique style of shooting from horseback. It was a deadly, efficient style that had been perfected and utilized by the Missouri guerrilla fighters under the command of William Quantrill and Bloody Bill Anderson. If that were true and John T. had been a member of that command, it was only logical that he could have known the Jameses and Cole Younger. It was common knowledge that they had all rode with Quantrill.

Placing the paper on the table and downing his drink, J.T. sat back in his chair and said, "Sorry, Abe. Didn't mean to ignore you like that."

Abe half smiled. "That's okay, John T. So they finally got the James boys, did they?"

J.T. shook his head. "No, not if that story is right. Jesse and Frank were the only two that got away. Charlie Pitts, Clell Miller and Billy Stiles were killed."

"How about the Youngers?" asked the Ranger.

Abe thought he saw water welling up in his old friend's eyes as J.T. answered.

"Posse caught up to them at a place called Madelia. They say Cole, Jim and Bob were nearly shot to pieces, but not dead. They took 'em back to Northfield, wherever in the hell that is."

J.T. paused a moment, then, as if thinking out loud, said, "What the hell were those boys from Missouri doing in Minnesota?"

"What most outlaws do, John T. Tryin' to rob a bank. Looks like they picked the wrong one this time," said Covington.

J.T. stared at the Ranger from over the top of his whiskey glass. "Outlaws," he called them. Maybe they were. But they hadn't started out that way. If everyone would have left them alone after the war, they wouldn't have become outlaws and they wouldn't have ended up bleeding and dying in some damn place like Minnesota. But no, there were those who wouldn't let the war go. They wanted vengeance against the men that had rode with Quantrill and Bloody Bill. The war may have been officially over, but it sure as hell wasn't forgotten. For some, it never would be.

There was a long moment of awkward silence at the table before Abe ask, "Anything ya wanta talk about, John T.?"

The gunfighter gave the question some thought. Abe Covington was a damn good friend, but he was still a Texas Ranger. He wondered what the lawman would do if he knew J.T.'d rode with Cole Younger and the James boys, not only during the war, but afterward as well. It hadn't been but two months ago that J.T. had sat in this very hotel and talked with his old friend and comrade-in-arms Cole Younger.

The outlaw had been glad to see that John T. was doing well, and reminded the bounty man that there was still paper out on him in Kansas and Missouri for his part in two of the James gang bank robberies that had occurred soon after the war. Cole had suggested that he restrict his chosen profession to the Nations and Texas. There was always the chance that someone in those two states might still recognize him, even after all these years. Turning the whiskey glass slowly in his hand, J.T. decided there was no reason to test his friendship with Abe by telling him about that time in his life. It was the past, and that was where it belonged. Not here at this table and especially not now.

"No, Abe. Thanks, like they say. Some things a fellow just can't talk about."

"Well, ya know where ya can find me if ya ever decide ya need to talk."

John T. smiled his appreciation and raised his glass. "I'll drink to that, friend. Thanks."

The two remained in the bar for another hour talking about the robberies and John Law's theory. Abe Covington had received two more telegrams after the bounty man had left the Ranger's office. One was a reply from Waco regarding more specific details on the robbery. Just as John T. had figured, they matched the Austin robbery in nearly every detail. The second telegram had come from the governor, who was presently in Washington trying to wangle federal money for Texas. Every paper in the north had picked up on the story of the robberies and cattle rustling that was going on in the state, placing the governor in a less than favorable light in the eyes of the nation's leaders.

The message had been clear, simple, and to the point. If Covington and his Rangers couldn't handle the trouble in that part of the state, the governor would fire the whole bunch and ask for federal troops to put an end to the lawlessness. He wanted this thing settled and damn quick. He was giving them an ultimatum. They had till the end of the month.

Over supper, J.T. told Abe he would be heading out at first light the following morning. From everything he'd seen and the telegrams in Abe's office, McLennan County appeared to be at the center of most of the activity that was going on. Of course he didn't have anything solid to hang his hat on that would prove any of that, but he had to start somewhere and Waco was as good a place as any.

"How many Rangers ya want to go with ya?" asked Abe.

"None," came the reply.

Covington dropped his fork on his plate and toweled his mouth before saying, "That's a goddamm good way to get yerself killed if ya run into anything up that way, J.T. Hellfire, we know there's gotta be at least thirty, maybe forty guns ridin' for this bunch. Could be even more'n that. An' here yer gonna go after 'em all by yerself."

Abe paused, tossed his napkin aside and shook his head.

"Yer good, J.T., no doubt about that. But there ain't nobody good enough to take on that many guns—not even you. I don't care if they do have yer damn watch!"

John T. pushed his plate aside. Leaning back in his chair he lit up a cheroot and smiled.

"Well, damn, Abe. I'm downright flattered you think I'd have the balls to try something like that."

"Flattered, my ass!" barked Abe with a slight grin. "Any damn fool who'd ride into the middle of an outlaw camp at night with guns ablazin' an' knowin' the odds were twelve to one is liable to do just about any damn thing. Balls! Hell, I don't know how you walk around without trippin' over the goddamm things."

John Thomas couldn't help but laugh at his friend.

"Now, J.T. I'm bein' serious here. Yer gonna need some help on this one."

Law put his cigar out and looked across the table. "I know, Abe. But I work better alone, you know that. Hell, I'm not even sure if I'll find anything to go on up there in Waco. But I promise you, if I do get on the trail of this outfit, I'll be calling on you for all the help I can get. You can count on that, okay?"

This seem to satisfy Abe Covington for the time being. "I got your word on that, right?"

J.T. raised his glass in a toast. "You just have your Rangers ready to ride when the time comes, Abe."

THE SUN HAD not yet broken the horizon when John Thomas Law walked the big buckskin, Toby, out of the livery stable and down the main street of Austin. What he'd told Abe was true. He had no idea what he would find in Waco. Maybe nothing. But all his instincts and experience seemed to be pushing him in that direction.

The news of the Northfield raid weighed heavily on his mind. Outlaws or not, those men were friends and former comrades-in-arms. Hard men all, they had played a rough and deadly game. Now some had paid with their lives, while others lay badly wounded and faced a rope or life in prison, and there was nothing he could do to help them. With fond memories of better times and a heavy heart, John Thomas Law, ex–Confederate guerrilla, gunfighter and bounty hunter headed north to Waco.

FIVE

✦

NEARING THE OUTSKIRTS of Waco, J.T. heard the sound of pounding hooves coming up behind him. Turning in the saddle he saw a stagecoach approaching, the leaders at full stride. From behind the rocking, bouncing coach, a long cloud of dust rose toward the sky as the driver snapped the reins and experienced hands urged the team on. Next to the driver sat the shotgun rider, who had one hand on his head trying to hold onto his hat, while in the other he held a tight grip on a short, double-barreled shotgun. The guard was keeping a close watch on J.T. as they quickly closed the distance on him.

"Reckon we better move off the road, Toby, 'fore that fellow runs us over."

With a gentle nudge of the knees, J.T. moved the buckskin to the side of the road. As rider and horse continued at a leisurely walk, J.T. reached into his coat pocket for a cigar. He was about to put fire to it when the thundering team of horses passed by. The shotgun guard nodded a greeting, but John T. hadn't even noticed. His full attention was diverted by the face of a blonde-haired angel who had leaned forward in the coach window and stared out at him as the coach came abreast of horse and rider. The stage was moving so fast that John T. had only caught a glimpse of her, but that was enough. In these few fleeting seconds he had taken in her beauty: corn silk hair, blue sparkling eyes and a cute little button nose. Almost the spitting image of Sara Jane.

In a hurried attempt to show proper manners, J.T. quickly brought his hand up to tip his hat and managed instead to look like an idiot. Forgetting about the cigar, he brought his hand up so fast that he broke the cheroot in half against the brim of his hat, which went flying off his head. In that small period of time she had seen it all happen and laughed, then smiled at him as the coach disappeared into a cloud of dust.

J.T. held his hand up to wave, then realized how ridiculous he must have looked, sitting on his horse with his hat in the dirt, his arm raised in the air and a broken cigar dangling from his hand. Shaking his head, he muttered, "Damn! I'd say that went rather well, wouldn't you, Toby?"

Tossing the broken cigar away, he stepped down and grabbed up his dust-covered hat. Slapping it against his leg, he stared at the fading dust cloud in the distance and wondered if that smiling angel was destined for Waco or simply making a stop before heading farther north. It had been a long time since he had seen a woman who impressed him as she had in those scant few seconds. She was definitely the kind of woman men only dreamed about. He could only hope that by some stroke of fate he might have the opportunity to somehow see her again.

Approaching Waco, the bounty man was amazed at how fast the place had grown, and from the looks of it, the expansion was far from over. The city had been named for the Waco Indians who had been the first inhabitants of the area. The Waco tribal village had been located a half mile from the Brazos River and was comprised of nothing more than a group of beehive-shaped huts, twenty to twenty-five feet high, made of poles, buffalo hides and rushes.

In the mid-1840's two enterprising brothers named Torrey established an Indian trading post on a bluff eight miles south of the village on the east side of the Brazos. A year later another settlement was built farther north by a rugged Scotsman named Neil McLennan, the man for whom the county had been named. In '46 Texas had become a state. Two years later, a group of businessmen from Galveston bought up all the land around the Waco village and with a surveyor began laying out the first streets and lots of what eventually would become the town of Waco. The property sold for five dollars a lot.

Among the first buyers had been a Texas Ranger named Shapley P. Ross. It was Captain Ross who had established a ferry across the river Brazos in '49 and built the first real house in the newly formed town. Like nearly all of Texas, McLennan County and Waco had suffered greatly following the War Between the States. The only thing that had saved Waco from becoming just another ghost town had been the ranchers and cattlemen to the south who had begun rounding up longhorns and driving the herds north.

In effect, one might say that it was John Chisholm who saved the town of Waco. As his cattle trail became more and more popular as a route, cowboys and their herds crossed the Brazos into Waco. Soon the town was making money left and right. More settlers began to arrive, businesses flourished and large cattle drives became a common site. By 1870, the city of Waco had built the first pedestrian/wagon bridge across the Brazos River.

It had been a mammoth project that had taken over two-and-a-half million bricks to build the 475-foot span across the river and brought the Texas section of the Chisholm Trail straight through Waco. A year later, the railroads reached the town turning the one-time Indian village into a hub of commerce for the state of Texas. It was plain to see why outlaws would find Waco and the surrounding counties so tempting. With the town's thriving economy, the place was a veritable treasure trove, with money flowing from cattle, banks, railroads and a continuous stream of settlers.

With thoughts of the young woman from the stage still on his mind, J.T. took Toby to the livery then walked the short distance up the street to The Ambrose. At one time the hotel had been the main place to stay in Waco, but now it was dwarfed by larger, more elegant hotels that had been built by the local tycoons. J.T. had considered trying out one of the newer places, but felt more at ease staying at a hotel he was familiar with. Signing the register at the front desk, he took his saddlebags and bedroll up to his room. Tossing the gear in a corner, J.T. sat on the bed and pulled off his boots. Swinging his feet around, he propped his pillow against the back of the headboard and was sound asleep in a matter of minutes. The kind of information he was looking for was going to require a lot of night work and a lot of saloons.

A FELLOW COULD learn a lot about the happenings of a town by simply setting at a table and listening to the talk going on around him. Saloons were a virtual gossip mill fueled by plenty of whiskey and loudmouth cowboys who often spoke without a thought of where they were or who might be listening.

Walking along the street, J.T. found there was no shortage of drinking establishments to chose from in this booming town. They had practically doubled in number since he had last visited Waco. As he made his way along the boardwalk he found there were some he could eliminate right away, like The Cattlemen's Club and The Baron's Emporium. These were exclusive establishments that catered to the big money and social magnets of the city. Hardly the kind of place one would find the everyday cowboy—or outlaw. No, the type of information John T. was looking for would be found in a saloon where the music was loud and the people were louder. A place like The Bull's Head.

As soon as he walked through the swinging doors he knew he was in the right place. It was crowded, smelly, smoky and loud. The piano player was pounding the keyboard for all he was worth. Big women, tall women, short women, women of all shapes and sizes sat on the laps of hard-drinking cowboys or stood sandwiched between two or three men at the bar. With hands groping their asses, the girls made sure that the boys doing the groping kept the flow of whiskey coming. When their money ran out, the girls would move on to a new set of hands. It was all part of the game. Faro and roulette wheels added their rhythmic clicking to the volume, mixed with the rowdy cheers of the winners and the moans of the losers. Looking around for a place to sit, J.T. noted that there were a number of professional gamblers dealing cards at different tables. It was another way of gauging the volume of business a saloon was doing. Professionals usually worked a deal with the owner for a percentage of the take from games each night. The Bull's Head had three working that he could see, a sure sign that business was good. As soon as a cowboy would lose his money and walk away, another stepped in to take his place.

Seeing no tables open, John T. was about to head to the bar when he noticed a man at a poker table in a far corner of the room raise his hand and wave him over. J.T. made his way through the crowd. Two men at the table stood up and walked away, leaving their money behind. J.T. thought the man who had waved looked familiar, but it was hard to tell. The smoke in the place was as thick as a Mississippi swamp fog.

When he neared the table he recognized the man. It was Charlie Beal, a professional gambler out of Arizona. Two years earlier Beal had saved the bounty man's life in a saloon in New Mexico. John T. had cornered the Hundley Brothers, two cold-blooded killers with nine dead men to their credit, three of them lawmen. J.T. had offered them the chance to give up, but knew full well they were not the kind of men to back away from a fight. When the fight came, there were only three shots: two from J.T. and one from Brit Hundley that went into the corner of the bar as he was falling. J.T. had walked over and knelt down next to the two dead men when a Hundley cousin appeared out of nowhere and grabbed a double-barreled shotgun from behind the bar. He would have blown J.T. Law's head off if it hadn't been for Charlie Beal, who drew and fired from his poker table, hitting the cousin squarely between the eyes.

After it was over J.T. and Beal had drinks and dinner. Talking long into the night, the two men became quick friends. Since that time, occasionally their paths would cross, with J.T. usually in pursuit of a wanted man, and Charlie working a poker table. It had been over five months since J.T. had last seen the gambler in a saloon in El Paso.

The gambler stood as J.T. approached. With a wide smile crossing his face, Beal reached out his hand.

"J.T. Law. How the hell are you, friend?"

The two men exchanged a firm handshake as J.T. answered, "Can't complain Charlie. It's good seein' you again."

There were two other men sitting at the table. One was a cowboy; the other was well dressed and judging from the talent he demonstrated shuffling cards, the man was another gambler. Beal released J.T.'s hand, pointed to an empty chair and offered him a drink.

"Sounds good, thanks," said John T. as he settled himself in the chair.

Filling a glass, Beal passed it across the table and began making the introductions, beginning with the cowboy.

"John T. this here is Josh Kincade. Josh is the foreman of the Circle H, one of the biggest spreads around these parts. Josh, this is J.T. Law."

Kincade reached across the table and shook J.T.'s hand. The grip was strong and friendly.

"Name's familiar. Pleased to meet you, Mr. Law."

J.T. was surprised to learn that this man was the ramrod of such a large outfit as the Circle T. He looked to be in his late twenties or early thirties. That was mighty young for a foreman. That was a title that was usually reserved for rock-hard, leather-faced old veterans in their late forties or fifties, but this Kincade fellow presented a clean-shaven, youthful appearance that was more befitting of a lawyer or bank manager.

"Glad to meet you," said John T.

Beal then turned his attention to the other man at the table, who had stopped shuffling the cards and was now staring across the table at the bounty man. Nestled between the expensive gray coat and double-breasted silk vest, J.T. saw the pearl-handled grip of a pistol in a shoulder holster. He figured the man to be in his thirties, but it was hard to tell for sure. The face was thin and drawn. The hair was light brown, almost as blonde as the neatly trimmed mustache that extended slightly over each side of the mouth. But it was the eyes that drew John. T.'s attention. They were cold, calculating, pale blue eyes that were staring at J.T., but keenly aware of everyone and everything around him.

"J.T. this is another old friend of mine. John Henry Holliday. Better known as Doc to most folks."

J.T. felt every nerve in his body suddenly come alive. He'd never met the famed doctor, but it was a name that was quickly gaining prominence, not only in Texas, but throughout the West as well. It was said that the onetime dentist turned gambler had killed nine men—some said more—in gunfights. He'd been labeled a cold-blooded killer by some, while others considered the doctor a well-mannered, well-educated Southern gentleman, who, given his profession and through no fault of his own, often found himself placed in situations that required steady nerves and a certain degree of proficiency with a gun. It just so happened the John Henry "Doc" Holliday had plenty of both.

Beal continued, "Doc, I take it you've never met . . ."

Holliday cut the man off and in a raspy, but quiet tone said, "John Thomas Law. I know. I've heard of you, sir. Can't say I care much for your line of work, Mister Law, but then, there are a considerable number of people that feel the same about me. I've been told you fought for the Southern cause. Is that true, sir?"

"You heard right, Mr. Holliday."

Holliday extended his arm across the table and the two men shook hands.

"Always a pleasure to meet a veteran of the cause, Mister Law. My friends call me Doc. Please feel free to do the same."

"Likewise, Doc. The few I have call me J.T."

The pleasantries exchanged, Beal poured another round of drinks and asked, "What are you doin' in Waco, John T.? Business or pleasure?"

J.T. was still studying Holliday. He had heard that Doc had tuberculosis and that he had come west for the drier climate. That would explain the drawn look about the face.

People also said that Doc could be as charming and well-mannered as any Southern aristocrat, but that when he was drinking heavy he became impetuous and surly in the blink of an eye. For the moment, Doc Holliday appeared to be perfectly sober, and went back to shuffling the cards in front of him.

J.T. lied, "Just passing through on my way to Dallas, Charlie."

It had just occurred to young Kincade who John Thomas Law was. A realization that seemed to make the ramrod nervous, a condition that was unmistakable in his voice as he said, "You're the man that tracked down and killed ol' man Baxter and his four boys, ain't you?"

"That's right, Mister Kincade. But it was the ol' man and three of the sons. Vigilantes took it upon themselves to hang the forth one. Damn shame, too. The kid was the only one of the bunch that was worth a shit."

Beal shook his head. "Goddamm vigilance committees. Never could figure out why a town bothered to hire a lawman if their damn committee was going to act as judge, jury and executioner anyway."

"People like to think of themselves as civilized, Charlie," said Doc. "A badge provides the appearance of legitimacy. A symbol of their trust in the law and the justice system. But they're quick to put those symbols aside for a night if things don't go the way they think they should. The vigilantes serve to correct what they consider the law's mistakes. If they want someone hung and they don't trust their precious law and the court to go that far, they take the law into their own hands, hide their faces and hang the poor sonofabitch themselves. When it's over, they walk away convinced that they've saved justice from making a mistake. Rather ludicrous, don't you think?"

"Reckon you're right, Doc," said Beal.

Kincade slammed his glass down on the table.

"Yeah, well, I wouldn't mind seein' a little more justice served up around here. Damn rustlers are stealin' the ranchers of McLennan County blind. Hell, we lost close to a thousand head the other day. I got two of my boys dead and three more shot all to hell. That makes five raids in the county over the last two months and we ain't caught a one of the bastards. Hell, we can't even find 'em, let alone hang 'em."

J.T. could see the frustration in Kincade's face. Judging from the way he had slammed his glass down, the young ramrod was well on his way to venting that frustration on a bottle of whiskey.

"What about the law?" asked J.T. "You got a sheriff, right? What's he doin' about all this trouble?"

Kincade laughed as he poured himself another drink. "Oh, you mean, Joe Wright—or maybe I should say, Sheriff Joe Wrong!"

This brought a belly laugh from Charlie Beal and even a slight grin from Doc Holliday.

"I take it this sheriff of yours is a little lacking in ability," said J.T.

"Yeah. That and the fact that the little fat bastard is lucky if he can find his way to the outhouse without gettin' lost," said Charlie between laughs.

Josh Kincade was about to make another comment, then paused. Looking over John T.'s right shoulder, he spotted the sheriff coming their way.

"Well, speak of the devil! Here comes the little shit right now."

J.T. turned slightly in his chair to have a look at the man who had been the point of discussion.

Sheriff Joe Wright was a short man, maybe all of five foot five, with big arms and chest and spindly little legs that gave him a hurried stride when he walked. The short little steps were almost comical as he approached the table. He had an old weathered gun belt around his waist, which was barely visible beneath an enormous gut that all but hid it from view. The face was plump and full, with sagging jowls. Two beady little eyes peered out from fat cheeks and bushy eyebrows. It was easy to see why few, if any, took the lawman seriously. Sucking in his gut as he neared the table, the little man attempted to pull his gun belt up an inch or two, but it slid right back down and disappeared under the massive gut again as soon as he exhaled.

J.T. could see why the man could easily become the butt of a conversation, but noted that there was nothing comical about the two deputies Joe Wright had with him. Both were big-sized men and had a hard look about them. One was carrying a short double-barreled Wells Fargo shotgun and he looked like he knew how to use it.

Kincade was just enough in the bottle to be feeling a little cocky. As the sheriff stepped up to the table, he said, "What's the matter, Joe Wright? Lose your way to the outhouse, did you?"

The lawman's fat cheeks puffed out and his face began to turn red as he barked, "Ya got a smart mouth, Kincade. It's gonna get yer ass in trouble one of these days."

The ramrod's face lost the grin as he set his glass on the table and stared hard at the lawman.

"Well, this is as good a day as any. You game, you fat sonofabitch?"

J.T. heard the twin hammers go back on the scattergun the deputy was holding and nodded to Beal, who quickly grabbed Josh's arm and held it firmly on the table, preventing the man from reaching for his gun.

Wright pointed a finger at the foreman.

"That there gamblin' man just saved ya from gettin' cut clean in half, Kincade. Now ya keep that damn smart mouth of yer's shut. I didn't come all the way over here to be puttin' up with no shit from a loudmouth drunk."

"Then just why are you here, Sheriff?" asked Holliday. "Is there a problem?"

Joe Wright's attitude changed in the blink of an eye. "Not at all, Mr. Holliday. It's just that with all the trouble we been havin' around here I told my boys to keep an eye out for any suspicious-lookin' strangers that come to town." Pointing to J.T., he continued. "They saw this here fellow and come got me. Just need to ask him a few questions, that's all."

Charlie Beal looked up at Wright. "You're the sheriff. The county is your jurisdiction, not the town. This is Marshal Heck Ramsey's territory. Why ain't he asking the questions?"

"Marshal's out with a posse. Got all his men with him. I'm just handlin' things till he gets back in the mornin'."

Doc Holliday leaned back in his chair. The left side of his gray coat fell to the side to reveal the pearl-handled pistol and shoulder rig he was wearing.

"So you believe this gentleman fits the bill as one of your 'suspicious characters.' Is that right?"

Little beads of sweat suddenly began to appear along the lawman's forehead. His deputies hadn't said anything about this stranger being a friend of Doc Holliday. The last thing Wright wanted to do was incense a man he considered a cold-blooded killer.

"Well, now, Doc. If this here fellow's a friend of yer's an' ya vouch for him, that's good enough for me."

Shooting an angry look at one of his deputies, he went on, "My boys should've looked into that 'fore they come for me. But, hey. No harm done, right?"

Doc glanced over at J.T. A slight grin broke at the corner of his mouth and he winked as he replied, "Well, I guess that's up to my friend here. Being classified a suspicious character may be an affront to the gentleman's character. Perhaps an apology from the law would be in order."

John T. knew Doc had the lawman on the hook and was having his own style of fun watching the little man squirm. But the two hard-case deputies were anything but amused by it all. The one with the shotgun took a step back from the table, leveled the scattergun in Doc's direction, and in a bitter tone said, "Why don't you go to hell, Holliday!"

The smile disappeared from Doc's face. His eyes narrowed. With his hands flat on the table in front of him, he sat upright in his chair. What had started out as out a joke was quickly getting out of hand. People standing behind the lawmen had overheard the comment made by the deputy and began to scatter out of the line of fire. Beal raised his hands slowly and whispered for Kincade to do the same, but the foreman was so drunk he totally failed to see the seriousness of the situation.

"Now who's fat ass is in trouble, Joe Wright?" laughed Kincade.

Beal quickly looked over at the cowboy and told him to shut up.

Joe Wright seemed confused by this sudden turn of events. How in the hell had this thing gotten so out of hand so fast? The saloon had gone as quiet as a cemetery. All eyes were on the table at the far end of the bar. Looking across the table, J.T. realized that all the stories he'd heard about Doc Holliday were true. The man had both barrels of a shotgun pointing straight at his head from less than ten feet away, but there he sat, calm, cool and collected, with both hands palm down on the table and those haunting blue eyes staring cold and lifeless at the man holding the scattergun. When he spoke, it was in a soft and clear voice.

"Mister Wright. I would suggest you rein in your watchdog, otherwise, if I see so much as a hair move on the back of his hand, I'm going to put a hole clean through that gun belt of yours before I die. Do we understand each other?"

Joe Wright was now sweating like a whore in church and his hands were visibly shaking. There was no doubt in the lawman's mind that Doc could do exactly what he said. Wright's first attempt at talking failed. His mouth was dry as cotton. His lips moved, but no words came out. Clearing his throat and wetting his lips, he tried again.

"Buck—now you lower that scattergun, ya hear me. Lower it and be damn careful how ya go about it. Do it now, boy."

The deputy kept the shotgun on Doc as he replied, "Hell, Joe. He's blowin' smoke. He ain't that damn fast."

"Goddamnit, Buck! Now do what I'm tellin' ya, boy! I mean it. Ain't no need for all this. Now lower that damn gun—now!"

Doc didn't bat an eye. He remained perfectly still, his eyes still fixed on Buck. J.T. wasn't sure if it was Joe Wright's plea or Holliday's lifeless stare that finally convinced the deputy to give ground in the standoff, but whichever it was, John T. was equally grateful. From his position at the table, he would have caught part of the blast from that scattergun.

Buck lowered the double-barrel and carefully dropped the hammers forward, much to the relief of Joe Wright. Buck slowly backed away from the table for a short distance, then turned and walked out the batwing doors mumbling to himself as he departed.

"Doctor Holliday, I'm sorry about that. Buck's a little high strung. I'll be talkin' to him 'bout that after I leave here," said the sheriff.

Doc didn't say a word. He simply kept looking at the lawman as if he were waiting for something. Joe Wright, still nervous, thought for a moment, then suddenly turned to John T. and said, "Uh, look here, mister, uh . . . uh . . . hell, I don't even know your name."

"J.T. Law." said the gunfighter.

Charlie Beal thought the sheriff was going to pass out on the spot. Wright's face went an ash gray and his voice was shaky as he ask. "John Thomas Law—the bounty hunter and gunfighter?"

J.T. nodded.

Swallowing hard, Wright forced himself to speak. "Mister Law, I'd like to apologize for my deputie's obvious poor judgment of character and I hope ya enjoy yer stay here in Waco."

Wright looked to Doc Holliday to see if his form of apology had been sufficient.

Doc smiled. "You have a good night, Sheriff. And thanks for stopping by."

The sheriff nodded, then quickly grabbed his other deputie's arm and hurried for the doors. The music and noise of The Bull's Head erupted again before the swinging of the doors had stopped. Everyone at the table, except for Doc, gave a sigh of relief. J.T. looked across at the man and shook his head as he said, "You cut that mighty fine, Doc. You really think you could have got that shot off?"

Holliday poured himself a drink. His hand was as steady as a rock.

"Guess we'll never know, J.T.—doesn't really matter now, does it?'

With his eyes drooping and slurring his words, John Kincade tried to say something. "Well, I th-think . . . Doc cou-could'a don-done it by Go-God. Yessss sirrr."

The ramrod never finished. His head pitched forward and banged hard on the table. The man had passed out cold. Beal shook his head. "Damn, I was hopin' he could stay on his feet long enough for me to get him over to the hotel. He's gonna be a load now."

John T. quickly downed his drink then offered to help Charlie get the cowboy to his hotel room. As the two men pulled the man up to carry him out, J.T. paused a moment and looked down at Holliday.

"Doc, you might wanta watch your back tonight. I don't figure that Sheriff's got the sand to try anything, but you made that Buck fellow look pretty bad in front of all these folks. Wouldn't put it past him to try and square that, first chance he gets."

Doc Holliday raised his glass in a salute.

"Your concern is admirable, my newfound friend, but I'm afraid Mister Buck will have to get in line with the rest of those with the same idea. If it should happen—so be it. See to your job at hand, John Thomas. I shall be fine, I assure you."

Charlie told J.T. that the Circle H maintained four rooms at the Waco Hotel year-round for business and travel purposes. It would be a good place to let the ramrod sleep it off. The two men managed to get Josh up the stairs and into the hallway. The clerk had given J.T. the key to one of the rooms. While Charlie struggled to keep the cowboy boss upright against the wall, J.T. worked the key trying to get the door open. Just as they were about to take Kincade inside, the door directly across the hall opened and both men found themselves staring at an attractive, full-figured woman in her twenties, with long blonde hair and a clinging while robe. John T. recognized her instantly as his stagecoach angel from this morning.

She stared at both men for a moment; then at Kincade. A strange look came over her face and she suddenly disappeared back into her room. Returning seconds later, she stepped out into the hallway holding a Colt .45 in her hands. Cocking the hammer back, she cried out, "Let that man go or I'll shoot!"

Beal and J.T. exchanged looks, then Beal tried to explain what was going on.

"Look here, ma'am. We're just—"

"I said let him go or I'll shoot. I swear to God I will," said the woman, raising the gun and pointing it in Charlie's direction.

Beal wasn't about to argue with a female who had her finger on the trigger of a loaded and cocked .45

"Well, hell, lady. I wouldn't want you to have to swear in public."

Taking Josh's arm from around his neck, Charlie let it drop and stepped aside. J.T. did the same. Josh Kincade wavered for a moment then fell forward facefirst in the hallway, hitting the floor with a terrible thud.

Watching the cowboy fall and hearing his head hit the floor so hard, the woman screamed out, "Oh, Josh!"

In her panic, the woman dropped the gun, which immediately went off, sending a bullet between Charlie's legs and into the wall.

"Jesus Christ, lady!" shouted the gambler.

But she didn't hear him. Rushing to Josh's side, she knelt down next to him and gently took his head in her hands. When she rolled him over, she let out a terrible scream. There was blood everywhere.

"My God! Did I shoot him? Oh, God!"

J.T. quickly knelt down next to her. He looked at the cowboy then answered, "No ma'am. He's not shot. He's just drunk. He broke his nose when he hit the floor. That's where all the blood's coming from."

Moving around to the other side, J.T. reached forward and popped the broken nose back in place. Sitting side by side with the woman, he caught the scent of roses from her perfume.

"There we go," he said. "Between the hangover and the busted nose, he's gonna wish somebody would shoot him in the morning."

While Charlie mumbled to himself and ran a finger through the hole in his pants that was only inches down from his crotch, J.T. asked, "I take it you know Josh, that right?"

She turned her face up to look at J.T. It was a beautiful face, as smooth and soft as a baby's bottom. Her blue eyes were the color of a Colorado lake in winter. The robe she was wearing had parted slightly at the top revealing the edges of her well-rounded, full breasts. God, she was beautiful.

"Yes. Josh is my brother."

Beal stepped forward. "Then you must be Lucy, from back east. Maryland, wasn't it? Josh talks about you all the time. But he never said anything about you coming to Texas."

She stood as she answered. "No, he didn't know. It was supposed to be a surprise. I was going to spend the night here and go out to the ranch tomorrow."

Charlie Beal, being the gentleman he was, quickly explained to the young woman that she shouldn't be too hasty in judging her brother's present condition. He assured her that Josh was normally a light drinker, but that things had not been going well at the Circle H the last few weeks and that the pressure on the young man had become so great that he had felt the need to let off a little steam. Had he known she was coming, there was no way that she would have found him in this condition. Not at all.

As Lucy Kincade listened to Beal's explanation, her eyes kept wandering over to John T. Each time he would catch her looking at him, she would quickly avert her eyes back to Beal. When Charlie had finished, she apologized for having shot a hole in his pants and thanked him for explaining the situation to her. It was easy to see that the gambler was as taken with the attractive young woman as John Thomas obviously was.

Looking at both men, she asked if they could please bring Josh into her room and put him on the bed. She would feel better if she could watch over him during the night and be with him when he woke up. Both men readily agreed that it was a good idea.

Charlie took his arms and J.T. took Josh's feet, and they carried him into the room. Lucy moved quickly ahead of them to turn back the covers. Placing Josh on the bed, Charlie pulled the man's boots off while J.T. undid the gun belt and placed it over a nearby chair. Once they were finished,

Lucy thanked them both and saw them to the door. As they were about to leave, Lucy looked at J.T. and said, "You look very familiar to me. Have we met before?"

John T. smiled. Reaching inside his coat, he removed a cigar, broke it in half and held it up in the air.

"Oh, yes." She laughed. "This morning along the road. Do you work for my brother?" she asked.

Lowering his arm, J.T. replied, "No, ma'am. I just met your brother this evening while he was in the company of my friend Mister Charlie Beal."

Charlie quickly snatched his hat off his head and nodded to the lady. "Pleasure to meet you, ma'am."

She smiled at Charlie, then looked back to J.T. "And your name, sir?"

"John Thomas Law, ma'am," he replied, removing his hat as well.

"Well, Mister Beal, Mister Law. I do so appreciate both of you looking after my brother. Thank you."

"Our pleasure, ma'am," said J.T.

"Glad we could be of assistance, Miss Kincade," said Beal.

Both men stepped out into the hallway as Lucy bid them goodnight and closed the door. As the two men made their way down the stairs, Charlie remarked, "That's gotta be the prettiest damn woman I've ever seen. An' I been a few places, friend, let me tell you."

"You won't get no argument out of me about that, Charlie. Kinda reminds me of another woman I used to know a long time ago."

As the two men stood on the boardwalk in front of the hotel, Charlie asked, "You headed back over to The Bull's Head?"

J.T. shook his head. "No, don't think so, Charlie. Might go back and get me some sleep. But let me ask you something. How long you been in Waco?"

Charlie leaned against a corner post and pulled out the makings for a smoke.

"Couple of months, I reckon. Why?'

"You heard any loose talk at all about these robberies or the rustling that's been going on?"

Charlie ran his tongue along the edge of the tobacco paper and slowly rapped his smoke. A halfway grin came over his face as he lit up and exhaled a long stream of smoke into the air.

"I didn't figure you were ridin' around the countryside for the hell of it, J.T. I imagine Wells Fargo and the railroad are offerin' up some pretty serious money for the boys that have been hittin' 'em lately. How much are you getting for this job, John T.?"

"A gold watch."

Charlie Beal looked confused by his friend's answer, but didn't press the matter.

"I haven't heard a damn thing, J.T. Whoever those boys are, they're stayin' pretty tight-lipped about their business. You got any idea who you're lookin' for?"

"No, not really, Charlie. I got this idea that these boys are all somehow connected to the military. You know, like former Rebs and Yanks. Everything they do is just too damn well planned and executed. Hell, the fact that you haven't heard a thing gives you an idea of how well disciplined they are. Whiskey'll usually loosen a fellow's tongue, but not these boys."

Charlie thought about what J.T. had just said.

"Well now, come to think of it. 'bout three weeks ago I was in a poker game with some fellows that were talkin' 'bout the war. One of 'em was a Yank and the other three were Rebs who had rode with Forrest. I remember thinkin' how downright civilized it was those fellows got along as well as they did, given the war and all. But they sure seemed friendly enough. Guess I didn't give it another thought. Hell, that war's been over a long time now, John T."

The bounty man's instincts came alert. "You remember anything they might have said, Charlie?"

The gambler puffed on his smoke for a few seconds then replied, "Damn, John, I been in a lot of poker games since then. But thinkin' back on it, I do recollect one thing I thought was kinda strange about that night. Two of the Southern boys were god-awful poker players. Lost just about every dollar they had. One of 'em got downright pissed about it, and started moanin' about how flat broke he was. The Yankee boy told him not to worry. They'd have plenty of change in their pockets once they got to San Antonio and hooked up with some fellow called Jack, or something like that. Let me see . . . No . . . It was Captain Jack—that was it. They'd be in the money once they found this Captain Jack fellow, whatever that meant. Sorry, John T., that's about all I remember. Wish I could help you out more, but they only played a couple more hands, then pulled out. I never saw 'em again after that night."

J.T. slapped Charlie on the back. "That's fine, Charlie. You might have given me more to go on than you think. I'll just have to see how it plays out. Think I'll turn in."

Charlie flipped what was left of his smoke into the street. "Sure you won't come over to The Bull for one last round? I'll buy."

"No, don't think so, Charlie. Doc provided about all the entertainment I can handle for one night. I'll see you tomorrow."

As J.T. walked away, Charlie said goodnight and headed across the street for the saloon. Halfway there he saw Doc come out the swinging doors. He was about to call to him, when Charlie saw two figures that had been lurking in the shadows of the alley next to the saloon suddenly rise up. Both men had shotguns and they were aimed at Doc Holliday. Charlie went for his gun, at the same time yelling a warning to Holliday.

"Doc! Look out—the alley!"

John T. had only gone a short distance up the street when he heard Charlie yell. Instinctively, the bounty man went for his gun. As he whirled about he saw Charlie Beal with his gun drawn and pointing toward an alleyway. In the same instant, Holliday dropped flat onto the boardwalk just as one of the shotguns roared. The blast missed Doc and hit two cowboys who were coming out the doors behind Doc. There were screams of pain as both men were blown back into the saloon by the blast.

Doc rolled off the boardwalk and into the street, where he snapped off two quick shots toward the alley. This brought a second shotgun blast, which tore up the dirt a few feet to the right of Holliday. Seeing his friend Doc was in a bad fix, Charlie rushed the men in the alley, screaming, "You bush-whackin' bastards!"

J.T. had both men in sight now and was about to shoot when Charlie ran directly into his line of fire. "Charlie, no! Get down!" yelled J.T.

But it was too late. One of the men leveled his shotgun at the charging gambler and let loose with both barrels. The impact of the blast picked Charlie up and threw him back-ward fifteen feet. He hit the ground like a shredded rag doll and didn't move.

Doc was on his feet now. "Goddamn you!" he screamed as he began walking toward the two men, delivering a hail-storm of lead into the alley. One of the assassins jerked sud-denly, then moaned as he dropped his shotgun and fell forward onto the walkway.

At the same moment, John T., his arm fully extended, sighted in on the second man and fired two well-placed shots. Both bullets struck the man in the chest and drove his body up against the wall. The man was already dead, but J.T. kept firing as he walked toward the alley, hitting the body four more times before it slumped to the ground.

Doc Holliday had reloaded by the time he joined J.T. at the entrance to the alleyway. Looking back at Charlie's shat-tered and torn body lying in a pool of blood in the middle of the street, Doc cussed out loud, "You sonsabitches!"

To the horror of the crowd that had began to flow out onto the street, Doc walked over to the body of the man on the boardwalk and fired six more shots into him. Reloading again, Holliday looked over at J.T. with those cold blue eyes as if expecting the bounty hunter to say something, but all he got was a nod of approval from the big man. Silently, they walked over to where Charlie lay. They had both lost a good friend.

Slowly, cautiously, the crowd began to gather, forming little groups to stare at the blood and mayhem that they had just witnessed. Amid the whispers and mumblings of the crowd, Sheriff Wright's high-pitched voice suddenly filled the street.

"What the hell's goin' on here? What's all the shootin' about?"

Someone in the crowd yelled out, "Couple of damn fools tried to bushwhack Doc Holliday."

"Are they dead?" shouted Wright, still trying to fight his way through the crowd.

"If ya mean the assassins—brother, they're as dead as ya can get. Doc and that fellow with him put a wagonload of lead in both of 'em," said a cowboy.

Holliday took his long gray coat off and placed it over one of the few real friends he'd ever had. The blue eyes were no longer threatening; now they showed only a marked sadness. Wright pushed his way to where the two gunfighters were standing.

"Who's that there?" asked the little man as he reached down to pull away the coat.

"You touch that coat an' I'll kill you," said Holliday in a matter-of-fact tone.

The crowd suddenly began to back away, realizing suddenly that this thing might not yet be over.

Wright looked at Doc. "Now look here, Holliday. The law says that I—"

J.T. interrupted the lawman. "You don't want to start no shit right now, Joe Wright. Neither one of us is in the mood. That's our friend Charlie Beal layin' there. If I was you, I'd do what Doc said."

Wright pulled his hand back, as he said, "Charlie Beal. I'll be damned. Sorry to hear that." Turning to Doc and John T., Wright said, "You two fellows are gonna have to come over to the jail with me till we can hold an inquest. An' I'll be needin' them guns, too."

Holliday ignored the sheriff. Seeing the undertaker standing in the crowd, Doc pulled a hundred dollars from his vest pocket and walking over to the man, whispered something, them gave him the money. A minute later, four cowboys gently lifted Charlie Beal's body and solemnly followed the undertaker to his office. All the while, Wright kept looking around in the crowd for his two deputies, expecting them to arrive at any minute.

"Now, Holliday, you an' J.T. Law here gotta go with me, you know that. So just hand over them irons. Judge'll hear the case first thing in the mornin'."

J.T. and Doc exchanged glances, then simply turned away and walked toward The Bull's Head. Surrounded by the crowd, Sheriff Wright knew they were all waiting to see what he was going to do. Screwing up his courage and puffing out his chest, the sheriff dropped his hand on the butt of his pistol.

"You two ain't special, ya know. Yer goin' to jail just like anybody else. Soon as I find my deputies, we'll be comin' in there to bring ya out. Now ya had fair warnin'."

J.T. stopped at the double doors and turned to face Wright.

"Sheriff, you won't have a hard time findin' your men— they're in that alley over there. Now, if you want to discuss it further, Doc and I will be waitin' inside until Marshal Ramsey gets back. We'll surrender our guns to him and nobody else."

Joe Wright felt his knees almost give out and his face turned a little green. Dammit, he'd told Buck to stay out of Doc's way and to forget about that business in the saloon. But Buck and his partner wouldn't listen. Now Wright had two dead deputies and near on to fifty witnesses that had saw them try to murder Doc Holliday from ambush.

Wright turned to the crowd and said, "Okay. That's fine with me. But if Ramsey's late getting back, one of you fellows tell them two bastards I said they had to be at Judge Bowers's courtroom in the mornin' at nine o'clock. It's a clear case of self-defense, but we gotta hold an inquest all the same. Some of you other boys, get the bodies of those two idiots over to the undertaker's. I gotta send a telegram."

Joe Wright hurried down to the telegraph office. The lights were out, but he banged on the door until the operator woke up and let him inside. Grabbing a piece of paper he wrote out the following message.

JACK CORBIN, CT RANCH. SAN ANTONIO, TEXAS
REGRET TO INFORM YOU OF SHOOTING THIS EVENING

IN WACO. STOP. YOUR MEN HARRY KLINE AND BUCK
TOBAN KILLED IN SHOOTOUT. STOP. WILL HOLD
BODY OF BUCK TOBAN UNTIL RECEIPT OF INSTRUC-
TIONS FROM BROTHER, DEKE. STOP.

JOE WRIGHT, SHERIFF, MCLENNAN COUNTY

SIX

✡

FRANK BOYD DUSTED himself off as he hurried up to
the main house. One of Jack Corbin's men had found him
at the corral and told him the captain wanted to see him right
away. Boyd had no idea why. Few men had ever been invited
to the main house for anything.

One of the Corbin's personal guards met him on the front
porch and took him inside. Pausing at the door to the study,
the guard knocked and waited until told to enter. Opening
the door wide, the guard motioned Boyd inside then stepped
out, closing the door behind him. Frank Boyd was instantly
overwhelmed by the room. It was outfitted with the finest
furniture and rugs he'd ever seen. Sitting directly in the center of the room was a huge mahogany desk with a high-
backed overstuffed chair. Along one wall, bookshelves filled
with books went from the floor to the ceiling. Fine artwork
in expensive frames hung throughout the room. Frank had
never seen anything like it and he doubted he ever would
again.

The cowboy had been so in awe of the place that he hadn't
noticed Corbin, instead focusing his attention on a huge por-

trait of naked women gathered around the ancient baths of Rome.

"Are you an art lover, Mister Boyd?"

The voice startled Boyd, who turned to find Jack Corbin standing behind him holding a glass of whiskey in each hand.

"Uh . . . sorry, Cap'n. I just never seen a room all this fancy before."

Corbin smiled pleasantly. "That's all right, Frank. I think every man should experience the finer things in life at least once." Corbin reached out his hand. "Here you go. From my finest stock. Have a seat, Frank."

Boyd took the glass and sat down in a fine leather chair positioned directly in front of the desk, while his boss took his place in the high-backed chair. Boyd took a sip of the whiskey. It was the best he'd ever tasted and it went down silky smooth. Resting the glass on the arm of his chair, the cowboy looked over at Corbin.

"What'd you wanta see me about, Cap'n?"

Corbin took a drink and set his glass aside.

"Frank, how long have you known Deke?"

"Long time, Cap'n. We rode together with Shelby's Brigade. Been close to fifteen years, I reckon."

"How about his brother, Buck?"

Corbin saw the cowboy wrinkle his brow at hearing the name.

" 'Bout five years, off an on. Never cared much for him."

"Really? Why's that, Frank?"

"Too damn cocky for me. Got a mouth on him, too. Deke's always makin' excuses for him, sayin' he's still young, that he'll grow outta that. But I don't think so. He's too hot-headed for his own good. Figure that's why Deke put him up in Waco with Harry Kline. Harry's pretty level-headed about things. Guess Deke figures Harry can keep the loudmouthed bastard outta trouble."

Corbin leaned back in his chair. "So what'd you think Deke would do if anything was to happen to Buck?"

The question put a knot in Frank Boyd's stomach.

"Damn, Cap'n. I don't even wanta think about that. Like I say, Buck's a sure enough pain in the ass sometimes, but he's still Deke's brother. Ain't no tellin' what he'd do. But whatever it was, it sure wouldn't be good, I'll tell you that. Why you askin'? Something happen to Buck?"

Corbin leaned forward and tossed Wright's telegram across to Boyd. Frank read it twice, then, shaking his head, placed the message on the desk.

"I'll be damned. Buck never was much of a gun hand. Knowin' him, I'd bet my saddle that wasn't no straight-up shootin' neither. Can't believe Kline let that hothead get him into somethin' like that. But won't matter how it happened, Deke'll want the head of the man that killed his little brother on a stick—an' he'll burn Waco to the ground if need be to get the man that did it."

A look of concern came over Corbin's face.

"That's what bothers me, Frank. So far we've been doing fine. Oh, we've had a few boys killed, but up to now, not a one of them have been caught, jailed or hung. That's why the law's out there running around in circles. They've never been able to put their hands on anyone to make them talk. Discipline, Frank. That's the key. Discipline and organization. But if Deke throws all that aside and goes off on some wild-ass spree because of this, there's no telling what could happen. Hell, he could endanger the whole operation."

Frank agreed. "Yes, sir. I'm afraid you're right. You know Deke'll wanta take all the boys with him when he goes to Waco. An' I think they'll go, Cap'n. They're pretty damn loyal to Deke."

Corbin stood up and began to pace around the room. He always could think better on his feet.

"We can't have that, Frank—not now. There are too many people out there looking for us. I may have been a little too ambitious these last few weeks, with the cattle raids, the bank and the railroads. It's almost certain the Texas Rangers are searching for any clues they can find. By now the railroads will have their own agents on the case. And we can't forget the reward money all of them are offering. No, we can't afford to draw any attention to ourselves right now. There's got to be another way to handle this."

Boyd sit silently turning his glass slowly on the arm of

his chair while Corbin continued to pace the floor. Frank didn't want to interrupt the captain while he was trying to work out this problem. There was little doubt in his mind that Corbin would come up with an answer. He had done good by them up to now and for a Yankee, Jack Corbin was a damn smart man.

As the minutes ticked by, Corbin poured himself another drink and went back to his desk. Looking at Frank, he said, "You said Deke wouldn't be satisfied with nothing less than getting his hands on the man that killed his brother, right?"

"Yes, sir, Cap'n, that's a fact. I know Deke. He won't let go of this thing till he puts that man in the grave."

A sly smile began to work its way across Corbin's face.

"Okay. Let's say he didn't have to go to Waco to find this man."

Boyd set forward in his chair. "I don't understand, Cap'n. What'd you mean?"

"Simple, Frank. We don't tell Deke about his brother—not just yet, anyway."

"Oh, I don't know about that, Cap'n. Deke finds out we—"

Corbin raised his hand to cut the cowboy off. "No, Frank. What I'll do is send you and some of the men to Waco. You find this man and bring him back here to the ranch. Once we have him on the ranch, Deke can do whatever he wants with the bastard and who's going to know?"

Frank was smiling now. He knew the man would come up with a plan. He always did.

"That's a hell of an idea, Cap'n. When you want me to head out?"

"The sooner the better. Pick your men. Tell them there's five hundred dollars a man in it for them. I'd like you to leave by noon, Frank. If Deke starts asking questions, tell him I'm having you move the north herd down to the river. How long do you figure it will take you to find this man?"

Frank was on his feet now. Placing the whiskey glass on the desk, he answered, "Shouldn't be more than three or four days. I figure our man Joe Wright can lead us straight to the

fellow. We hogtie him and head back the same day. I don't
see no problem, Cap'n."

Corbin seemed pleased with the cowboy's answer. Reaching across the desk he shook Frank's hand.

"I can see I'm sending the right man for this job, Frank.
There'll be another glass of that whiskey waiting for you
when you get back."

Boyd thanked the man for the vote of confidence and
headed for the door. Just as he was about to leave, Corbin
called out.

"Frank?"

Boyd turned, "Yes, sir?"

"You might want to pick some of the boys that are especially handy with a gun. Joe Wright didn't say who killed
Buck, but remember, Kline was with him too, and they're
both dead. Just a thought."

Frank nodded, "Yes, sir. Nothing wrong with a fellow
having an edge. See you in three or four days."

Frank hurried out of the room, closing the door behind
him. That business taken care of, Corbin opened the center
desk drawer and took out a letter he had been reading when
Frank Boyd had arrived. The letterhead bore the stamp of
the Texas Legislature. Corbin focused on the portion of the
text that had excited him the first time he had read the letter.
Silently, he read it to himself again.

*Having met in secret this evening and presented your pro-
posal, the head of the nominating committee has assured me
that your offer of a $75,000 contribution will be more than
sufficient to secure you a nomination for attorney general on
the first ballot.*

The letter was signed by the senior-ranking member of the
house who had placed a postscript below his name instruct-
ing Corbin to destroy the letter after he read it's content.
Reading that portion again, Jack Corbin couldn't help but
laugh. They must think I'm a backwoods fool, he thought to
himself. Placing the letter back in the envelope, he stood and
walked across the room to Gainsborough's portrait *Blue Boy*.
Pushing the frame aside to reveal a wall safe, Corbin placed
the letter inside and spun the dial. That letter could prove

useful once he made his bid for governor of Texas. Jack Corbin's dream was progressing nicely. He was not about to let anything interfere with his carefully laid plans, especially a dead brother who, from the sound of things, probably got what he deserved.

FRANK BOYD STEPPED off the porch and headed for the bunkhouse. There was an added spring in his step. He had just had a meeting with the head honcho of this outfit. The man had expressed a high degree of confidence in him and even shared his expensive whiskey with him. Taking care of this little problem for Jack Corbin could be a big feather in his cap. Might even move him up in the organization to a top spot like Deke's.

As he rounded the corner of the bunkhouse, Frank saw a dozen or so men gathered at the corral. It was Tom Duggan and his crew. They were just returning from Mexico where they had sold the stolen herd from the Circle H. Duggan was a Yankee like Corbin and the captain's second in command. But it wasn't Duggan who Boyd was interested in at the moment, but rather two of the men in his crew. One was Choctaw Jones; they called him Breed. He was a half-breed Mexican and Apache who was quick with a gun and as mean as a bag full of rattlesnakes when he was riled. The other was Quincy Cole, a former member of the Sam Bass Gang who had a reputation of his own as a gunmen. It was said that Cole had killed seven men in straight-up gunfights. Frank believed it. He had seen the man shoot. It was Cole's deadly accuracy that had accounted for every one of the dead Circle H riders the day they stole the herd. Frank knew he still needed to pick three more men, but these two were a good start. He walked up just as Choctaw Jones was about to pull the saddle off his horse.

"Breed, you an' Cole hold onto them saddles and pick out fresh mounts."

Jones turned and looked at the man, then giving him a go-to-hell look, tossed his saddle up onto the top rail of the corral fence as he said, "I'm too damn tired for your jokes,

Frank. Gonna get me some grub, then sleep for two days straight."

"You are jokin', right, Frank?" asked Cole.

Boyd leaned back against the corral fence. "No, I'm not. Gotta get three more of the boys and be on the road for Waco by noon."

Jones and Cole exchanged glances, then both shook their heads.

"Hell no, Frank," said Cole, "we been in the saddle for three damn days straight. Ain't no goddamn way I'm getting back on a horse. Not till I had me some sleep."

"Same goes for me," said Breed.

Frank stepped away from the fence and shrugged his shoulders. "Okay. Fine with me, boys. I guess I'll just have to find a couple more fellows who want your five hundred dollars to make the trip."

Boyd hadn't gone three steps before Cole called out. "Hey, Frank. Wait a minute. That five hundred dollars a piece?'

Frank turned on his heels. "That's right, Cole. Five hundred a man. We ride to Waco, get this fellow the cap'n wants to see and ride back here. That's the deal. Now you boys want in or out?"

"Damn, Breed. Sounds like easy money to me," said Cole.

Breed nodded. "Yeah. That's what worries me."

"Okay, Frank. We're in. But you gotta get somebody to saddle us some mounts while me an' Breed get something to eat."

Frank agreed and told them to go ahead, he'd take care of that. He'd have them rigged and outfitted by the time they were through. Assigning that task to a couple of the men at the corral, Boyd went into the bunkhouse and found three more men he knew were handy with a gun and told them to get ready to leave. Duggan witnessed the activity and asked Boyd what was going on. Knowing that there were too many men standing around that might overhear, Boyd told Duggan he'd have to talk to the captain about the details.

Within the hour, Frank Boyd and his crew were ready to ride. They were about to turn out and head for the main gate when Deke rode up. Frank followed Corbin's instructions and gave Deke the story about moving the north herd. Cole and Breed heard the lie then looked at each other questioningly, but didn't say anything. Hell, for five hundred dollars, Frank could tell Deke whatever he wanted. Having no reason to doubt Frank's word, Deke told him he'd see him later.

Leading his men out the main gate, Frank felt guilty about having lied to his friend and even more guilty knowing Deke's brother was dead and not saying a word. But he was sure Deke would overlook all that once he handed over the man who had killed Buck. Or at least he hoped he would. Taking out his newly acquired fine gold watch, Frank noted the time. Twelve noon on the dot. The captain would like that. It showed organization. Smiling to himself, Frank closed the watch and slipped it back into his vest pocket. Now all they had to do was go get a man in Waco and bring him back—how hard could that be?

SEVEN

★

MARSHAL RAMSEY ARRIVED back in Waco with his posse just after dawn. Before he had a chance to step down from his saddle, no less than five citizens had rushed out to tell him of the overnight events and the fact that Doc Holliday and J.T. Law were still holed up in The Bull's Head saloon refusing to turn over their guns or come out until he had returned. Dismissing the citizens in the posse, the bone-weary and saddle-tired marshal sent one of his deputies to wake the sheriff and bring him to the saloon. He told the other deputy to take down the statements of the five people who had told him what had happened. While that was going on, Ramsey reined in at the hitching post in front of the undertaker's. Dismounting, he beat on the door until the man finally woke up and opened the door. The lawman wanted to see the bodies of the men killed.

Marshal Heck Ramsey was a man who took his job seriously. A big man in his late forties, he stood just over six foot, had a stout frame and big hands. The face was wrinkled and weather-worn, a roadmap of sorts that bore the lines of a man who had spent his life more in the elements than in the comfort of an office. The hair was salt-and-pepper black and he had a thick, bushy mustache, which all but hid his upper lip. He was a little more than upset as he viewed the bullet- and buckshot-riddled bodies of the men in the back room. He had been appointed town marshal to put a stop to just this kind of murder and mayhem. The fact that three men had been killed in the streets of Waco was nothing more than an affront to the law and his personal authority.

Of course, he hadn't even been in town when this had happened, but to Ramsey that didn't matter. It was his town and as the chief law official, he felt responsible for everything that happened in the Waco city limits. The fact that Doc Holliday and famed bounty hunter John Thomas Law were involved was sure to garner a wave of newspaper reporters not only local, but nationwide as well.

But as upset with the situation as he was, Heck Ramsey was not only a professional lawman, but a fair one as well. If, like the five witnesses had said, this had been a clear-cut case of self-defense, he would do all in his power to see that Doc Holliday and J.T. Law were acquitted of all charges of wrongdoing in this affair.

Waiting on the front step of The Bull's Head saloon for Sheriff Joe Wright to arrive, Ramsey found one thing in particular troublesome about the shooting. Two of the dead men were sheriff's deputies. Joe Wright had hired them three months ago. They were not local Waco residents and no one, including himself, knew anything about either one of them. Ramsey had found it rather strange that Joe Wright would hire two men who even he admitted he didn't know that much about. Especially that younger one, Buck Toban. Ramsey had only had dealings with the man a couple of times when he had become involved in a few barroom brawls and two shootings that were questionable. But those few times had been enough to convince the veteran lawman that Toban was a loudmouthed braggart and a dangerous man to pin a badge on. But he was only the marshal of Waco—not the overseer of McLennan County. That was elected Sheriff Joe Wright's responsibility and Ramsey couldn't tell the man who to hire or who to fire.

Ramsey heard the muffled sounds of grumbling and complaining as Joe Wright made his way around the corner and headed for the saloon. He was upset at having been awakened this early in the morning. As the marshal watched him approach, Ramsey wasn't sure if Joe Wright was just a poor judge of character or if perhaps he really did know Toban and this fellow Kline. If so, why hide it? And what about the rustling? Was he really as inept at his job as he appeared? Questions and more questions. It always seemed to come out that way whenever it came to the happenings around McLennan County and the county's elected peace officer. This business last night had done little to resolve that.

The two lawmen stood out in front of the saloon. Wright gave the details of the shooting as he knew them and pointed out the various locations where the action had taken place. When asked about the involvement of both of his deputies, Wright quickly pointed to the minor altercation that had occurred earlier at the poker table. He had no idea that the two men would go so far as to try and bushwhack Doc Holliday. They had acted solely on their own and had paid the price. As far as Wright was concerned, it had been self-defense. But the refusal of both men inside the saloon to surrender their weapons and accompany Wright to the jail was another thing altogether. The sheriff wanted them arrested for that reason if nothing else. The marshal ignored the request.

Walking to the double doors, Ramsey called inside and told Doc he was coming in to talk things over with them. There was no need for any more shooting. Holliday assured him there wouldn't be any. Ten minutes later the three men walked out of the saloon and went to the marshal's office. Joe Wright noted that both gunmen were still armed, fact that he took as a personal slap in the face from Ramsey, and one he wouldn't soon forget.

Once in the office, J.T. asked if they would still have to appear in court. The marshal told him no. Between all the witness statements, his viewing of the bodies and the scene of the altercation, along with Wright's own claim that it was self-defense, Ramsey felt he had more that enough to satisfy the judge. An inquest would only be a waste of time. Ramsey did, however, inform both men that even though they hadn't started the trouble, he preferred that they conclude their business in Waco by the end of the day and leave town. It was almost certain that news of the shootout was spreading far and wide across Texas by now and it was sure to draw an element that could only cause trouble as long as both men remained in Waco.

Joe Wright had followed the group to the office and now smiled as he stood to the side and waited to see what Ramsey would do when these two gunfighters told him what he could do with his request. But the smile was quickly lost as Doc and J.T. thanked the lawman for the professional way he had handled the situation and told him that they would both be leaving before the day was over. Ramsey nodded his approval and assured both men that as far as the law was concern this matter was closed.

Doc and J.T. left the office and headed for a hotel restaurant for breakfast. As the waitress brought them coffee and took their order, J.T. asked, "What are you going to do now, Doc?"

Before Holliday could answer, he began to cough. Pulling a kerchief from his vest pocket he pressed it to his mouth and continued to cough, each time more violently than the last. When it finally stopped, J.T. thought he saw spots of blood on the kerchief as Doc folded it over and put it away. Doc then answered the question as if nothing had happened.

"Oh, hell, I was ready to leave anyway. Deck's been cold the last few days. Think I'll head up to Fort Griffin and deal a few hands at Shanssey's, maybe lay up with a bottle and a whore till the luck falls my way again. How about you? Did you find what you were looking for already?"

J.T. smiled. "So you didn't buy that story about passing through did you, Doc? Didn't fool Charlie either."

Doc took his finger and ran it around the rim of his coffee cup.

"I'm going to miss Charlie. We had some damn good times together. I kind of figured you were looking for information about those robberies the other day. Was Charlie able to help you out?"

J.T. set his fork aside and stared at Holliday. "I'm not sure,

Doc. He gave me a name. Somebody called 'Captain Jack.' That name mean anything to you?"

Doc shook his head. "Can't say it does, J.T."

Law went on to tell Holliday his theory of a gang comprised of ex-military men. When he had finished, Doc said, "Interesting theory you have there, John T. I'd have to say its more than a theory. Kind of reminds me of another outfit. They were all ex-military men when they first started as well. Of course, you know who I'm talking about."

J.T. shifted in his chair, suddenly feeling a little uncomfortable about where this conversation was going. Doc gave a slight grin.

"That's all right, John. No need to worry. I spent a lot of time in Kansas. Remember seeing an old reward poster for the James Gang. Figure it must have been an early one because the reward money wasn't all that much at the time. Let's just say there was a description on that poster of a fellow that could pass for your twin brother."

"You think so, Doc?"

"I know so. Like you said, men that drink in saloons have a habit of talking too loud and often too much. But we've all got something from our past lurking in the closet and we all try to hide those old ghosts. But you know, sometimes that's not a good thing. Correct me if I'm wrong, but didn't the James Gang operate virtually in the same manner as the group you are looking for? Perhaps a look back into the past may be warranted to find some possible answers to the present. Only a thought, of course."

J.T. was surprised to find that Doc Holliday would know so much about him. But he had a good point. Jesse, Frank and Cole had began their outlaw ways using the tactics that they had learned during the war. And for a time their outfit had consisted of nothing but ex-military men who could ride, shoot, and obey orders without question. Doc was right. That past was a mirror image of the present situation. Although J.T. had only participated in two bank robberies back then, he had spent countless hours listening to Jesse and Cole describe possible targets, lay out extensive, detailed plans for the raids, as well as precise instructions and landmarks designated as escape routes. J.T. now felt certain that somewhere within all of those memories were more than a few that could possibly give him an edge on the men he was after.

"Thanks, Doc. I hadn't thought of that, but you're right."

Holliday was about to say something else when he sat upright in his chair and his face beamed. His attention was focused on the front door of the restaurant.

"I do declare, I've never seen a woman in this wilderness who could hold a candle to a Georgia girl until now. Stunning! Absolutely stunning."

J.T. turned slightly in his chair and glanced at the front entrance. Josh and Lucy Kincade were just entering. Josh still appeared a little shaky on his feet. Both eyes were swollen and turning black and blue from the broken nose, but at least he was up and moving around. As for Lucy, Doc was right— stunning was the perfect word. She had her long golden hair pulled back and wrapped with a bright yellow ribbon that matched the color of her form-fitting yellow dress. Her blue eyes seem to sparkle amid the field of yellow.

J.T. caught their attention and waved the couple over to join them. Doc looked questioningly at the bounty man.

"That's Josh Kincade's sister. Her name is Lucy. She came in on the stage yesterday."

Doc quickly rid himself of the cigar he had just lit, straightened his coat and vest then quickly stood as the couple arrived at the table. J. D. stood as well and made the introductions. Always the gentleman, Doc pulled out a chair for the lady whose soft voice and sparkling eyes all but melted both the hardened gambler and gunfighter on the spot. Once all were seated, Josh and Lucy both expressed their condolences. They had heard about the shooting death of Charlie Beal before leaving their hotel. Lucy still couldn't believe it. She had just talked with the man less than twenty-four hours ago and now he was dead. It was a stark reminder for her that she was no longer in the civilized bastions of the east.

The couple ordered breakfast, then Josh said, "They say you got both of the bushwhackin' bastards."

"Josh! Watch your language. You are in a public place.

This is a restaurant—not one of your rowdy barrooms," scolded Lucy.

The gunfighters looked across the table at one another and grinned as they watched the ramrod of the biggest spread in McLennan County drop his head, slump back in his chair and utter an apology to his sister.

So as not to prolong Josh's embarrassment, J.T. quickly answered the question.

"That's right, Josh. It was Wright's deputies. Doc and I both dropped one."

Josh's eyes lit up. "Damn! I'd've loved to seen that."

The comment brought another stern look from Lucy.

"I fail to see anything beneficial in witnessing the death of two men. If anything, people should be horrified at such a spectacle."

"Ma'am, I assure you, Mister Law and I took such action only in defense of our person. The two men in question left us no choice in the matter. I might add that the local law enforcement and court have agreed with us on the matter," said Holliday.

J.T. nodded in agreement. "He's right, Miss Kincade. If Charlie hadn't warned Mister Holliday, he would be a dead man right now. I know you don't have this kind of thing going on back east, but out here a man is on his own when it comes to defending himself."

Seeing that she was not about to win any type of argument as far as western justice was concerned, Lucy directed her attention to Holliday.

"Doctor Holliday, if I may ask, with what field of medicine are you associated?"

Doc's face seem to take on a gentle glow.

"The field of dentistry, ma'am."

Lucy smiled as she said, "Oh, so you have an office here in Waco, then?"

"Well, no, ma'am. I had an office in Dallas for awhile, but I'm afraid certain health problems have resulted in my having to forego the profession at this time."

"I'm sorry to hear that," said Lucy with true sincerity.

Josh looked at his sister and laughed as he jokingly said,

"Yeah, sis, you might say Doc's still pullin' teeth, but now he does it with a deck of cards."

This brought a laugh from the other two men at the table as well. The group continued to talk until the waitress arrived with the couple's order. Doc suggested that he and J.T. leave them to their breakfast.

"Meeting you has been a most pleasant experience, Miss Kincade. Perhaps one day we will meet again," said Doc as he stood to leave.

Lucy smiled at Holliday. "Thank you, Doctor Holliday. I have enjoyed our conversation immensely. You are a very interesting man, sir."

"And you as well, ma'am. You coming, J.T.?"

"Sure, Doc," said J.T. as he stood. "Josh, I'd like to talk to you before you head back to the ranch. Maybe we could meet later."

"Sure, J.T. How about our hotel, about noon?"

Law told him that would be fine. They both bid the two men farewell as they left the restaurant. Lucy commented, "That man, Doctor Holliday, is such a pleasant man. Well educated and highly articulate as well. Did you notice that he managed to carry on that entire conversation without having to cuss once? That's the kind of person you need to be spending more time with, Josh. Not those foul-mouthed, brawling cowboy friends of yours."

Josh almost spit out his coffee. Setting the cup down, a grin crossed his face as he said, "I don't think so, sis. Doc Holliday's killed ten men, and that fellow with him, John Thomas Law—at last count—nineteen. I don't think Mom and Dad would approve."

Lucy was shocked. Turning in her chair and looking through the window she watched the men cross the street.

"My word! And they seem like such perfect gentlemen."

"Hell, sis. A .45 don't care what kind of manners a fellow has."

AT NOON, J.T. was on his way to his meeting with Josh when he saw the foreman pull up in front of the hotel driving a handsome buggy rig. Hopping down from the seat, Josh saw the bounty man coming his way and waved a greeting.

"Hey, J.T., I thought Lucy might be more comfortable riding out to the ranch on something with springs instead of a hard-ass saddle."

Law grinned as he replied, "I'm sure she'll appreciate that, Josh."

"Where's Doc?" asked Josh.

"Doc pulled out about an hour ago. Headed for Fort Griffin."

Josh nodded, "Yeah. An I'll bet Marshal Heck Ramsey had a big part in his decision to pull out."

"You'd win that one, Josh. Matter of fact, he asked us both to be movin' on. Marshal's a fair man, though. Can't really blame him none for wanting to keep the peace," said J.T.

The two men went into the lobby where Lucy's luggage sat. Grabbing up the bags, they carried them out and loaded them onto the buggy. While they waited for the young woman, the two talked about the sudden rash of rustling that had hit McLennan County. J.T. had a number of questions for the ramrod. Was there anything in particular that stood out about these raids? Josh couldn't think of anything other than the fact that all the rustlers were expert horsemen and damn good with their shootin' irons.

Why hadn't anyone managed to track them down?

Josh explained that following the trail of these outlaws had proven to be a risky business. Two other outfits had tried that and ended up riding straight into ambushes that had cost the lives of more than a few cowpunchers. That had pretty much discouraged anyone else from trying their luck at tracking them.

"What about the law? Didn't they try and track them down?"

"Oh, sure. Joe Wright and his boys would ride around the county for a day then come back with a dozen different reasons why they couldn't find anyone or anything. When we got hit a week ago, Marshal Ramsey took it on himself to go after the bunch. That really seemed to upset Joe Wright.

He went screamin' to the judge and the city council about jurisdiction and all that shit. When the marshal and his boys came back, the judge called Ramsey to his office and really laid into the lawman pretty good, from what I hear. Never did hear if they found anything, but they were gone nearly four days."

J.T. found this bit of information interesting. Why would a man like Joe Wright, who appeared obviously inept at his job, kick up so much dust about getting some much-needed help from a highly professional and experienced lawman like Heck Ramsey?

Lucy came out of the hotel as that thought crossed J.T.'s mind. He tipped his hat.

"Afternoon, Miss Kincade."

She nodded. "Mister Law. Nice to see you again. Are you coming out to the ranch with us?"

Josh looked to the gunfighter.

"Now there's an idea, J.T. Since you gotta get out of . . . uh . . . I mean, since you were leaving town this afternoon anyway, why not come out to the Circle H with us? I'm sure the general would like to meet you and we could talk some more while I showed you around the place."

John T. considered the offer. For the moment all he had to go on was a name that went with a place somewhere around San Antonio. Neither of which meant anything for the time being. And he still had a lot of unanswered questions about Sheriff Joe Wright. The man was either a complete idiot with a badge, or a sly fox who wanted people to think him a fool. J.T. wasn't sure which.

He had come to Waco in the hope of finding some answers, but so far all he had managed to accomplish was losing a friend, meeting another gunfighter and killing a man. Instead of answers, he now had even more questions. The only saving grace up to this point had been meeting Josh and Lucy Kincade. Perhaps Josh was right. He couldn't stay in Waco anymore. Hell, if Doc Holliday took Ramsey's request serious enough to get out of town, who was he to ignore it? By accepting the offer he would have a place to stay while he took a couple of days to do some investigating on his own. It would also allow him to spend some more time in the company of Lucy Kincade.

Josh helped his sister up into the buggy, then climbed in beside her. Settling into the seat and picking up the reins, he looked at J.T. and asked, "Well, whaddya say, J.T.?"

"Thanks, Josh. I appreciate the offer. I'd kind of like to meet the general. I've heard a lot about him. Why don't you two go ahead. I've still got a couple of things to take care of here before I leave. I'll catch up with you."

John T. Law's acceptance seem to please Lucy.

"Okay, then," said Josh. "Just take the south road out of town. Main house is about seven miles out. You can't miss it."

Popping the reins, Josh headed the buggy out of town. J.T. watched them to the end of the street, then turned and headed for the marshal's office. The door was open. Walking inside, he found Ramsey at his desk looking through a stack of wanted posters. A deputy sat at another smaller desk in the far corner, cleaning a rifle. Both men looked up as J.T. entered the room. A frown came over the marshal's face as he tossed the poster he held in his hand aside. Leaning back in his chair, Ramsey fixed his eyes on the bounty hunter. The deputy nodded to J.T. and went back to cleaning the rifle.

As J.T. crossed the room toward the marshal's desk, Ramsey said, "Good afternoon, Mister Law. I'm surprised to see you're still here. Figured you might have rode out with Doc this morning."

J.T. stopped a few feet in front of the desk.

"Doc and I are headed in different directions, Marshal. But I'm on my way out of town now. I just had a couple of questions. If you got a minute, I'd be obliged."

The news that the gunfighter was on his way out of town eased the frown, but was quickly replaced by a look of curiosity. Pointing to the chair next to his desk, Ramsey replied, "I reckon I got some time. Have a seat."

J.T. dropped down into the chair as the man asked, "What can I do for you, Mister Law?"

"Well, Marshal, since you know who I am, then you know the business I'm in."

There was a clear hint of sarcasm in Ramsey's voice as he replied, "Yeah, I do. Bounty hunter. Can't say I care much for the profession."

That didn't seem to bother J.T. "Not many folks do, Marshal. Especially the men you got on those flyers there."

Ramsey glanced at the pile of wanted posters on his desk. The man had a point. Men like J.T. Law served a purpose for the time being, anyway. There were simply more bad men and outlaws in the state of Texas than there were lawmen to track them down.

Heck Ramsey's distaste for bounty hunters had come from having to pay out reward money for wanted men who were brought in slung over saddles and with bullet holes or buckshot in the backs. There was just something about it that didn't sit well with the lawman. True, they were wanted men and it was the state that had put the price on their heads, dead or alive. Still there was something about backshooting a man, even an outlaw. Ramsey felt that every man deserved a chance to stand up and die like a man. Even a wanted man.

From all he had heard about the bounty hunter sitting at his desk right now, J.T. Law was one of the best in the business. A man who was respected by lawmen and outlaws alike for his courage and sense of fair play. It was that distinction that separated this man from the others, and the primary reason Heck Ramsey had agreed to take the time to talk with him.

"What is it you'd like to know, Mister Law?"

"Let's say I've got a friend who's asked me to look into this business of the train robberies and the rustling that's been going on the last few months."

"Okay. We can say that if you want. Other than the fact that I'd like to catch the sonsabitches myself, how does that concern me?"

"I understand you took a posse out on your own after the Circle H raid. I'd like to know if you found anything while you were out there."

Ramsey gave a grunt as he shifted in his chair. That was a decision he had made that he would not soon forget. The judge's ass-chewing and the city council's reprimand still left a bad taste in his mouth. Leaning forward and placing his elbows on the desk, Ramsey laid out the events of that day.

Upon receiving word of the raid, he had waited to see what action the sheriff would take. As usual, Wright had taken his posse that morning and returned that afternoon saying they couldn't find anything. Tired of the sheriff's excuses, the marshal had taken it upon himself to do his own investigating, knowing full well that he would be out of his jurisdiction. Selecting a posse of handpicked men, they had quickly found the trail and set out in pursuit. From the signs they'd found, Ramsey figured that they were after at least twelve to fifteen rustlers. Acutely aware of the ambushes faced by previous outfits, he had put two of his best men out on point and two more to the left and right as flankers. That precaution had paid off on the second day. Ramsey's flankers came up on a group of men laying in ambush for the posse. A short gun battle had ensued in which a couple of his men had been nicked, but nothing serious. The rustlers had broken and run after keeping the posse pinned down for nearly an hour. They continued to follow the trail south for three days and could have gone on if they had been better supplied. But going after the rustlers had been a hurried decision on Ramsey's part and they didn't have the supplies or resources to continue the chase. Reluctantly, he had returned to Waco. It had been that decision on his part to take a posse out that had almost cost him his job.

J.T. had listened closely to every word. "So you and your posse didn't have any trouble picking up on the trail as soon as you got out there, is that right?"

"That's right. Hell, it'd be damn hard to hide a trail when you're pushin' nearly a thousand head of cows. A blind man coulda followed them fellows."

J.T. leaned back in his chair as he said, "But Joe Wright and his boys couldn't find anything to go on. Don't you find that a little suspicious, Marshal?"

Ramsey nodded. His face was serious as he replied, "Hell, there's a lot of things that worry me about Joe Wright. Like those two deputies of his. One day they just show up. Nobody know anything about 'em. They're not from around these parts, then two days later, they're sheriff's deputies. A week later, all this rustling business starts and Joe Wright can't find his ass with both hands—even a trail as wide as the damn Mississippi. Yeah, you might say I got a problem with the sheriff of this county. I take it you got your own ideas about the man."

J.T. looked the lawman straight in the eye. "I just find it curious that every outfit that's went out after this bunch has been ambushed and shot up somewhere along the trail—every one that is but Joe Wright and his boys. If I didn't know any better, Marshal, I'd say you have a sheriff that's working hand in hand with these rustlers."

Ramsey leaned back in his chair. There it was. Somebody had finally said what he had been thinking for a long time now. Joe Wright was on the payroll of the rustlers. That would explain the money. Over the last few months, Joe Wright had been spending far more than he made for being sheriff. That, tied in with all the rest, made it look pretty bad for the lawman. As much as it troubled him to admit it, he felt J.T. Law was right.

"Sayin' it and provin' it are two different things, Mister Law. But I can promise you this. You find something to back up that idea of yours an' I'll arrest Joe Wright myself."

"If he's involved, Marshal, I'll find out in the long run and hold you to that. By the way, have you ever heard the name Captain Jack?"

Ramsey thought about it for a minute, then shook his head. "Can't say I have. Think this fellow might be involved in all this?"

"Yeah, I do. Got the name from Charlie Beal. Way he made it sound, this Captain Jack could be the main ramrod behind this outfit. Can't seem to find anyone who's ever heard of him, but I will."

"Sounds like you're takin' this personally, Mister Law," said the Marshal.

J.T. told him about his experience with the gang on the train and about losing his gold watch. He described a few of the men he'd seen during the robbery, especially the man with the scar across his nose who had taken his watch. It

was the watch and the picture of the girl inside that had made
it personal.

J.T. got to his feet. Extending his hand across the desk,
he shook hands with Ramsey.

"Thanks for your help, Marshal. I'll be staying out at the
Circle H for a few days. I find anything, I'll let you know."

For the first time since meeting this man, Ramsey showed
a friendly smile.

"Do that, Mister Law. If I can be of any help, be sure an'
let me know."

J.T. thanked the man and left. Across the room, the deputy
worked the lever on the rifle a few times then stood and
placed it in the rifle rack. Looking over at Ramsey he said,
"Never thought I'd see the day Heck Ramsey would be
shakin' hands with a bounty hunter."

Ramsey walked over to the coffeepot sitting atop a pot-
belly stove. Filling his cup, he turned to the deputy and in a
somber voice replied, "I never thought I'd meet a bounty
man I respected more than a sheriff either."

EIGHT

★

BEFORE LEAVING WACO, J.T. stopped by the telegraph office and wired Abe Covington.

    CAPT. COVINGTON. RANGER HGS. AUSTIN, TX.
    NEED INFORMATION ON FOLLOWING NAMES. STOP
    CAPTAIN JACK STOP HARRY KLINE STOP BUCK TOBAN
    STOP WILL BE AT CIRCLE H RANCH NEXT FIVE DAYS
    STOP FORWARD ANY INFORMATION AS SOON AS POS-
    SIBLE STOP.

                                    J. T. LAW, WACO, TX.

Picking up Toby at the livery, J.T. headed out on the south road. Giving the big buckskin his head, he spurred Toby on, allowing the horse to stretch his legs. In no time they had caught up with Josh and Lucy Kincade. The trio carried on a conversation for the next couple of miles. A short time later they arrived at the main gate of the Circle H. Two cowboys were just on their way into town when they saw their boss and the attractive young woman by his side. As one shouted a greeting to the couple, the other studied the man in black riding the buckskin. He had seen the big man somewhere before but couldn't remember where at the moment.

"Hey, boss. We were just comin' into town to find you," said the young cowpuncher. Walking his horse up to the buggy, he noticed Josh's black eyes. "Damn, boss, what happened?"

"I'll mind you to watch your language there, Bob. There's a lady present," said Josh, smiling at his sister.

Young Bob quickly snatched the dusty hat off his head and apologized.

"Lucy, this is Bob Nelson and that rough-lookin' ol' man over there is Jed Davis. My right-hand man when I'm not around. Gentlemen, this here is my sister, Lucy."

Having heard his name mentioned, Davis shifted his gaze off J.T. and to the young woman. Tipping his hat he greeted the lady, then looked back at the man in black.

"Don't I know you, mister? Your face sure seems familiar," asked Davis.

Before J.T. could answer, Josh cut in with a comment.

"I don't think you'd want this fellow knowing you too well, Jed. This is John Thomas Law, the bounty man."

In the blink of an eye the situation around the buggy took a serious turn. On hearing the name, Jed Davis uttered the word, "Damn!" and slapped leather, but before his gun cleared the holster, he heard the hammer go back and found himself staring down the barrel of J.T.'s Colt Peacemaker.

"Let that iron drop back in that holster, friend. I don't really wanta kill anybody today if I don't have to," said Law in a matter-of-fact tone.

Josh was on his feet, standing up in the buggy. He shouted to Davis, "Do as he says, Jed. That's an order." Out of the corner of his eye Josh saw young Bob easing his hand toward his pistol, and barked, "Damnit, Bob, that goes for you, too. What the hell's wrong with you, Jed? What's this all about?"

Davis released his pistol and let it drop back into the leather. "It's personal, Josh. But you got my word. Long as this man's your guest here, there won't be no more trouble. Looking hard at J.T., Davis snapped, "But once you leave here, Law, we got some settlin' up to do and don't you forget it."

Yanking hard on the reins, Davis turned his horse and rode back toward the bunkhouse. J.T. eased the barrel of the Peacemaker toward Bob. "You got anything to say? If so, get it done."

The young cowboy slowly placed both hands on his saddle horn and shook his head from side to side as he answered, "No, sir. I know for a fact we ain't ever met. I was just worried about Jed, that's all."

"Bob, why don't you head on back to the house and let the general know we're comin'," said Josh.

Bob nodded. Tipping his hat to the lady again, he wheeled his horse and rode for the house. Lucy, her hands still shaking, looked at J.T. and asked, "Would you have shot that man if he had pulled his gun?"

J.T. lowered the hammer on the Colt and slid it back into place.

"Yes, ma'am. Just as sure as you're sittin' there."

She seemed stunned by his answer. "So you would kill a man for no other reason than the fact he may have a grievance with you. Is that right?"

"That's absolutely right, ma'am."

"But you don't even know what that grievance is."

J.T. shook his head, as he replied, "That's right, Miss Lucy, but it wouldn't matter much what it was if I was dead now, would it? Least this way I still have a little time to find that out what's bothering Mister Davis. I can tell you this: I've never seen the man before in my life. So I got no idea why he's got a burr under his saddle. But I intend to find out."

Josh settled himself back in the buggy as he said, "Well, that's the first time I even seen Jed act like that. One thing for certain, he's never broke his word to me. If he says there won't be any trouble long as you're here, you can believe that. But I hope you two can work it out before you have to leave. Now, what'd you say we go to the house?"

As the trio made their way to the main house, John T. kept trying to place Jed Davis. But he was getting nowhere. Like he had told Lucy, he'd never seen the man before. The same was true of the name. Josh had told him not to worry, Jed Davis was a man of his word—of course that was easy for him to say, he wasn't the one who had been threatened. Man of his word or not, John T. knew he was going to have to stay alert during his visit to the Circle H.

Josh reined in the buggy at the front steps of the huge ranch house. Tom Harrison, former ex–Confederate general, Texas legislator and cattle baron came out onto the front porch to greet his foreman and guests. Tying off his horse at a hitching rail next to the house, J.T. made his usual bounty hunter evaluation of their host. He figured the man to be in his mid-fifties and close to six feet tall. Dark hair was beginning to gray on the sides, but only added character to a strong and rugged face. The eyes were brown, and at the moment, bedazzled by the beauty of Lucy Kincade.

Skipping down the steps with the exuberance of a man half his age, Harrison greeted his foreman. Noting the black eyes, he showed honest concern as he placed his hand on Josh's shoulder.

"Looks like you been buttin' heads with a buffalo, son. You all right?"

Clearly embarrassed, the young foreman replied, "Yes, sir. Ran into a floor with my nose. But I'll live. Sorry I was gone so long."

Harrison laughed. "That's all right, son. I done my share of floor kissing, too. Thought I recognized those trademark eyes the minute you drove up."

John T. laughed along with the others. He could tell right away he was going to like this man.

"General, I'd like to present my sister, Lucy. She's come all the way from Maryland to pay me a visit. If it's not too much trouble, sir, I'd like for her to stay in the main house while she's here."

Harrison stepped forward and taking the young woman's hand in his own, raised it up and gently kissed it, then replied with a smile, "By all means, Josh. It would be a honor. Been a long time since we've had such beauty and grace in our humble abode."

Harrison had easily won over the young woman with his southern grace and charm. For the first time since meeting her, J.T. noticed a slight blush appear in her cheeks. Her smile and silky-smooth thank-you only served to charm the old general even more. Calling for two of the house servants to escort Lucy and her luggage to one of the guest rooms, Harrison told her to make herself comfortable. He would send the maid to her room to help her freshen up and get situated. Lucy thanked him again and followed the servants inside.

"General, this is J.T. Law. He helped me out after my little dance with that floor I was tellin' you about."

Harrison's eyes looked J.T. up and down from head to toe. Reaching out, he shook J.T.'s hand with a firm, friendly grip as he said, "Oh, yes. Mister John Thomas Law. I know the name well. You might find it flattering to know, sir, that your name has been mentioned in the halls of the Texas State Legislature on more than one occasion."

Now it was J.T.'s turn to blush as he smiled and replied, "If you don't mind my asking, General, is that a good thing or a bad thing?"

Harrison released the gunfighter's hand and laughed out loud.

"Leery of politicians are we, Mr. Law? I can assure you, my boy, you are held in high esteem among many of the members of the Texas House. We figure if we had a few more good men like you we could rid ourselves of every bad man and scandal in the state. We were particularly impressed with your handling of that murderous Baxter Brothers business a few months back. It's a real pleasure to finally meet you, sir."

J.T. was temporarily at a loss for words. He was so used to having people looking down on him and his profession that actually hearing something positive coming from a man of Harrison's stature had momentarily left him stunned.

"Well, we're in luck then, General," said Josh. "Mister Law here has been asked by a friend to look into the latest robberies and rustlings that've been going on around here."

This news peaked Harrison's interest. "That right, son?"

"Yes, sir. Captain Covington and I discussed the problem down in Austin."

Harrison smiled. "Ol' Abe. He's a smart one, all right. I sent him a telegram about a week ago asking for three or four Rangers to be sent up here to help us out. Seeing as how he sent you by yourself, I'd say that says a lot about your ability, sir. You got any ideas about all this, Mister Law?"

"Yes, sir. I do," said J.T., with a hint of well-deserved pride.

"Well, let's go inside and have a drink while we talk about that."

Josh signaled for two cowboys to come up from the corral. Once they were there, he told them to take care of J.T.'s horse and to have someone take the buggy back to the livery in Waco. That taken care of, the trio moved to Harrison's library where the host poured them all a glass of his finest bonded whiskey. Taking seats in a series of high-backed chairs arranged in a semicircle around the fireplace, John T. led off the conversation by telling the two men of his theory in regards to the makeup of the gang that was rising havoc throughout this part of Texas. He then suggested that from what he'd seen and heard since his arrival in Waco, there was a very good possibility that Sheriff Joe Wright was somehow involved with the gang.

The general nodded his head as he said, "I've been having a few thoughts along that line myself. However, I heard about what happened the other night. I fail to see why Wright would have his deputies ambush Doc Holliday. What could that possibly have to do with all this trouble?"

"Absolutely nothing, sir," said J.T. "That was a personal thing between Doc and one of the deputies. But it shows that Wright had no control over either one of the men who were supposed to be working for him. That shooting caused a lot of problems for Wright that I'm sure no one knows anything about. If those men, Kline and Toban, were members of the gang working with the sheriff, then he's going to have to do some explaining to somebody about what happened to them. For all I know he may have already done that."

"Well, as far as I'm concerned, that little sonofabitch is up to his fat-ass neck in this thing. I just know it," said Josh.

"You may be right, my boy, but knowing it and proving it are two different things altogether," said Harrison. "We have to have solid evidence to back that claim."

"I say we grab up the bastard and beat the hell out of him till he tells what he knows," said Josh.

Harrison frowned at hearing this. "That won't do, Josh. There's laws and they have got to be followed. We go grabbin' up people an' torturing them until they say what we want to hear, then we might as well give Texas back to the Indians. What if we were wrong about Wright? What then? How would you justify what you did to the man? No, son. It's all got to be done legal and proper using the law and the evidence."

Josh's frustration with the legal process exploded.

"Well, that tears it then! Hell, this outfit's been raiding up and down the line from Waco to San Antone' for near on to a year now an' there ain't nobody come up with anything. It's like we're chasing a bunch of gawddamn ghosts. Evidence! Hell, you want evidence? I got two hard-working, honest cowboys buried out there in the damn yard. The Box XT has two. Mike Brown's outfit's got four—just how many more have we got to put in the ground before you put your precious law aside and go after people like Joe Wright? They either talk or we string 'em up to the nearest tree. Trust me, General, we do that an' sooner or later somebody'll talk. I'll guarantee that."

J.T. could understand Josh's anger. He had to admit, the idea of grabbing Joe Wright and scaring the hell out of him to make him talk had crossed his mind. But stringing the man up, that might be taking it a little to far.

"Calm down, Josh," said the bounty man. "Getting yourself all worked up here is not going to accomplish anything. We've got to outsmart them. Put together some kind of a plan. Going off half-cocked won't do anybody any good. We've got to figure a way to turn the tables on this bunch."

"Be a neat trick if you can pull it off, son. You got any idea how to go about that?" asked Harrison.

"No, sir, not at the moment. But give me a little time to think on it. I'm sure there's a way, I just got to figure it out. I sent a telegram to Abe asking him for some information. I'm hoping he'll come up with something. By the way, General, you ever heard the name Captain Jack?"

Harrison thought for a moment then shook his head. "No. Can't say I have. Why?"

"I'm not really sure what it means. It's just a name I picked up along the way. It could be nothing; then again it could be the name of the leader of this bunch."

Harrison stood, finished his drink and set his glass on the table.

"Well, gentlemen. We can discuss this more a little later. For now, what do you say we get ready for dinner? I for one am looking forward to dining this evening with the prettiest girl in Texas."

"I totally agree, sir," said J.T.

Josh, his temper cooled, raised both hands. "Okay, you fellows. Please. You keep this up you'll have that girl's head so high in the clouds nobody back in Maryland will be able to live with her when she goes home."

The comment brought a round of laughter from the three men as they left the library. Harrison had one of the servants show J.T. to his room. He was a guest. Anything he might need he had only to ask one of the servants. Dinner would be served at seven.

NINE

⬟

SHERIFF WRIGHT REACHED into the metal cash box he kept locked in the bottom drawer of his desk. He counted out fifty dollars.

"This better be worth every damn penny, Bill Jenkins, or y'all be findin' yer ass behind them bars 'fore the sun sets."

The tall, lanky man with the pockmarked face and visor on his head watched the lawman count out the money as he replied, "Now, Joe. Have I ever steered you wrong? Hell, you boys been doin' all right with my information about those train schedules and gold shipments. Fifty dollars for special information ain't all that damn much. Not for what I got here. I think you'll find it interestin'."

Slapping the money into the man's hand, the sheriff growled, "All right. Ya got yer money, now give me the damn thing an' get back to the telegraph office."

Jenkin's tossed the copy of J.T.'s telegram onto the desk. Shoving his money in a shirt pocket, he hurried out of the office.

Opening the paper up, the first words to catch Joe Wright's eye were ABE COVINGTON AND TEXAS RANGERS.

"Dammit!" uttered the sheriff.

When he had finished reading he laid the wire on his desk
and stared at it for a long time. How in the hell did J.T. Law
come up with the name Captain Jack? The only people that
used that name were Corbin's men, and Wright knew they
were the most tight-lipped bunch he'd ever met. The other
thing that had him concerned was Law's request for information on Kline and Buck Toban. There were fifty Rangers
working out of Austin. Those men roamed far and wide, their
duties taking them through every little town and village
across South Texas. During their travels, they talked to a lot
of people. It was good odds that someone in that Ranger
outfit had crossed trails with Buck Toban or at least had
heard his name mentioned in casual conversation. It wasn't
going to take Covington or one of his Rangers long to link
Buck with his brother, Deke—a man suspected of robbery
and murder in Kansas and the Indian Territory. Wright was
convinced that it was that link that was going to eventually
lead straight back to him and his possible connection to Deke
Toban.

This fellow J.T. Law was no fool. He couldn't have sur-
vived as long as he had if he was. Once he made the connection and went after Deke the trial was going to lead him
straight to Captain Jack himself and then there was going to
be hell to pay. Joe Wright had no desire to get caught up in
the middle of all that. But what should he do? His first im-
pulse was to take the money Corbin had paid him over the
last year and disappear. But he really didn't want to do that.
He had a lot of that money invested as a silent partner in
three of the biggest saloons in Waco. Between Corbin and
the lucrative profits from the saloons, Joe Wright was doing
damn well for himself. There had to be another way.

Drafting a telegram explaining the situation and its possible ramifications, Wright ended by asking Corbin what he
should do about the problem. Taking the message to Jenkins
later that night, he told the operator to send the message
"Special." This indicated that Jenkins was to code the message using a system that had been developed by Corbin himself. Like Wright, Jenkins was on Captain Jack's payroll.
And they weren't the only ones. The enterprising Corbin had

eyes and ears in practically every county from Dallas to the Mexican border. It was little wonder the law was having problems pinning the bunch down. Hell, they knew what the law was going to do even before they did.

Understandably worried, but confident he had done all he could, Joe Wright went home and went to bed. Jack Corbin was the man with all the ambition and the answers—let him work out the details.

Twenty miles from Waco, six men crossed Santa Rosa Creek and stepped down from their horses once they were all across. Frank Boyd and his crew had decided to make camp for the night. They would head into town in the morning for their meeting with Sheriff Joe Wright.

AT THE CIRCLE H, dinner had gone well. Harrison had his staff serve up a veritable feast while he entertained his guests with exciting and sometimes exaggerated tales of the early days of the founding of the Circle H Ranch. After dinner they all retired to the front porch. A gentle warm Texas breeze greeted then as they took their seats. Drinks were served while a trio of Mexican guitarists serenaded them with some of the general's favorite music.

Lucy had been bombarded with compliments from the moment she had entered the dinning room, and she had loved every minute of it. The young woman could not remember a more gracious host than Tom Harrison. The compliments, the wonderful dinner and a fine wine served with the soft, gentle strumming of guitars in the background—it was all so wonderfully overwhelming. She now realized why her brother had never expressed an interest in ever returning to Maryland.

Shortly after ten, Harrison bid his guests goodnight and retired to his room. Not long after, Josh rose and give his sister a kiss on the cheek and thanked her for coming to see him. Telling J.T. goodnight, he too retired for the evening, leaving the pair alone on the porch, the musicians having departed earlier.

"Would you care for more wine, Miss Kincade?" asked J.T.

"Yes, please. If you don't mind."

J.T. filled her glass and passed it back to her. As he did so, their fingers touched. He expected her pull her hand away, but she didn't. Their eyes met. In her soft, sultry voice she said, "Thank you, Mister Law."

"The name is John Thomas. Most folks just call me, J.T. That Mister Law thing sounds a bit formal. But of course you can call me whatever you like, Miss Kincade."

A sly grin formed around her lips and spread across her face.

"Now, I'll bet that's an offer you make to very few people."

"You have a point, ma'am."

"And my name is not ma'am. It's Lucy."

"Okay, Lucy."

"Okay, John."

They both laughed. Touching glasses, Lucy made a toast. "To Texas."

J.T. raised his glass. "To Texas."

The couple remained on the porch talking until midnight. Normally not one to talk about himself, J.T. found it impossible not to do so where this woman was concerned. Before he knew it, he was telling her about his parents and their move to Texas, the family ranch and how it had been lost during the war. When asked if he had served during the conflict, J.T. had limited his reply to a simple, "Yes. On the side of the Confederacy."

She studied him while he talked. He was a handsome man with just enough of a rugged edge to make him interesting. The blue-green eyes seemed to change depending on the topic of conversation. When speaking of his parents the eyes were soft and gentle, just as they had been when he had come to Josh's aid in the hotel that night. On the subject of the war and the loss of the ranch, they took on a hard, almost threatening look. She concluded that they were the eyes of a man who had seen more than his share of violence. The voice could be soothing and soft or as threatening and hard as the stare. She had seen a perfect example of that at the main gate during the confrontation with the cowboy Jed Davis. He was certainly a complex man, but a man who she found herself strangely drawn to each time they met. She couldn't explain it. Maybe it was the smile when he laughed as he had done a number of times listening to the general's stories, or perhaps it was the strong feeling of safety she felt whenever she was in his presence, the feeling that nothing or no one could harm her as long as he was near.

What was wrong with her? She was a woman who hated violence, yet she felt this strange attraction to a man who kept company with other gunman. A man that had supposedly killed nineteen men—twenty, counting the man in Waco. Part of her was afraid of him, but it was the hint of that fear that excited her, made her feel so alive. As he continued to talk, she suddenly found herself trying to imagine what it would be like to have his lips on hers. To feel his big strong hands hold and caress her as no man had ever done. All kinds of wicked thoughts began to fill her mind. She suddenly felt so very warm. She was out of control. Quickly jumping to her feet, she uttered, "Oh, my!" then began to fan herself feverishly.

With concern on his face, J.T. stood and reached out for her as he asked, "Are you all right, Lucy?"

He was so close. His firm hands were holding her arms. She looked up into his eyes and knew she had to get away from him before she did something she would regret later.

"I . . . I have to go in. Goodnight, John."

She pulled free of his hands, turned and almost ran into the house, leaving J.T. standing alone trying to figure out what he had done to cause such a reaction from the woman. Pouring himself another drink he strolled to the porch swing, which hung at the end of the house, and sat down. Sipping at the whiskey he stared out at the vast, star-filled sky and said to himself, "I swear, I don't think I'll ever understand women."

"If you ever get it figured out, let the rest of us men know, will you?"

J.T. looked to find Harrison in a robe with a cigar in one

hand and a drink in the other. "Mind if I join you?'

"No. sir. What's the matter, General, couldn't sleep?"

Harrison took a seat in a chair next to the swing. "No. Haven't been sleeping right since all this trouble started. Hearing Josh talk like he did tonight kinda adds to it, I guess. I know he means well, but I worry about him and that temper of his. Can't help it."

"Boy's got a hair trigger, I'll give him that," said J.T.

"It was that temper that got him out of Maryland and transplanted here in Texas to begin with."

"I was meaning to ask you about that. Josh is a fine fellow, but he seems a little young to be ramroddin' an outfit this size. Especially since I've seen a lot of older hands that look like they been around quite awhile. Men like that Jed Davis, for example."

Harrison took a puff off his cigar and blew a long column of smoke into the night air. "Yeah, Jed's been with me since the war. He was a sergeant in my command. He can be a crusty old bastard sometimes, but he's a good man. As for Josh, well, let's just say I owed his father a favor—not the job of foreman, mind you; Josh earned that on his own. How that came about is kind of a long story. But now if you were getting ready to retire I won't keep you."

J.T. shook his head. "No, sir. I wasn't plannin' on turnin' in for awhile yet. I'd kind of like to hear the story."

This seemed to please the old general, who suddenly excused himself and went back into the house. A minutes later he returned and handed J.T. a tintype picture of a Yankee colonel in full dress uniform. John T. saw the likeness right away.

"That there is Josh and Lucy's father, Colonel Jacob W. Kincade. A colonel in the Army of the Potomac. That picture was taken near the end of the war. If it wasn't for that man there, me, Jed Davis and half the other boys you see workin' around this ranch wouldn't be alive today."

J.T. studied the picture for a moment then said, "I can see this is going be an interesting story, General."

As he began the story, Harrison sit back in his chair, his eyes not looking directly at J.T. but rather into the darkness as if they were reliving the past while he spoke.

It was the final days of the war. Harrison's command was one of the last Confederate forces of any substantial size remaining. They had been cut off and surrounded by troops of Colonel Kincade's cavalry. Three days of bitter fighting had left Harrison's force in a shambles with over seventy percent either dead or wounded. Knowing the war was lost and would end any day, Harrison could no longer stand watching the suffering of his troops. Reluctantly he raised the white flag of surrender to put an end to the battle.

But Kincade's commander, a general who harbored a bitter, deep hatred of the South and its Rebel army refused to accept the surrender. Instead, he sent Harrison a message that the battle would be to the death and no quarter would be given. Nearly all of the Yankee officers within the command were outraged by their commander's action, but fear of the general, who had demonstrated that he had no problem placing disloyal officers in front of a firing squad, led only to whispered protest.

As the Yankees readied their troops for the final charge that would roll over the beleaguered Rebels, the general reminded his troops he wanted no Rebel prisoners taken, the extermination of this last remnant of the Southern cause was to be total and complete. What the Yankee general conceived to be a rally speech, his own soldiers considered an abortion. They, like their officers, knew that Lee was finished. For all reasonable purposes, The War Between the States was over. There was no need for this needless slaughter. But they feared their own commander and the consequences they would face if they left even one Southern soldier alive.

It had been Colonel Kincade who had finally stepped forward to voice protest against the order. His loyalty to the Union was immediately attacked by the general in front of the entire command. Enduring a savage assault upon his character, loyalty and courage by the general, Kincade waited until the man had finished then informed him that as the senior-ranking officer in the field, he was relieving the general of his command for medical reasons. When the general had laughed at him and asked what medical condition, Kincade's reply had been loud and clear for all to hear.

"Because you, sir, are fucking insane!"

The details of what happened next varied among those who were there, but basically what happened was that the Yankee general drew his pistol and fired two shots at Kincade before the colonel calmly drew his own pistol and ordered the general to lower his weapon. The man refused and prepared to fire at Kincade a third time. Both men fired at the same time, more in the fashion of a duel than a gunfight. Kincade was hit in the arm, the general in the heart.

The general dead, Kincade proceeded to call forth a major, his next in command, and turned over his pistol, putting himself in the major's custody. This brought a wave of protest from the soldiers. The officers conferred for a time then returned the pistol to the Colonel, loudly proclaimed that the general had been killed by a Rebel sniper and that he was now in command. Each and every soldier there swore an oath that they would never reveal the actual events of that morning.

Shortly afterward, Kincade advanced alone with a white flag and conferred with Harrison. Within an hour they had negotiated an honorable surrender. Horrified at seeing the condition of Harrison's badly tattered army, Kincade immediately had the Southern wounded attended to by his medical staff and saw to it that badly needed food, water and blankets were provided to every Rebel soldier. Although these things were certainly appreciated by the Southern men, it was Kincade's dignified treatment of General Harrison and his refusal to accept the Southern gentlemen's sword that had endeared the Yankee colonel to the Rebel troops.

Lee surrendered to Grant two days later. The war was over. However, Kincade maintained a hospital in the area until he was certain the wounded were well enough to go home or were able to be moved by their comrades. Kincade even provided horses and wagons for that purpose. Tom Harrison was overwhelmed by the man's sense of honor and compassion. Before parting company, Harrison had told Kincade that as long as he lived there could be no favor too great to ask of him, and that he and his men would be forever indebted to him. He had saved their lives.

The two men had remained friends, exchanging letters off and on over the next five years. Then two years ago, Josh had let his temper get the best of him and he had killed a man in a barroom brawl. Everyone agreed that it had been an accident. Josh had hit the man and the fellow had hit his head on the corner of the bar rail when he fell. This was the first time Josh had been in trouble. For that reason the colonel felt that this time the State of Maryland had had enough of Josh Kincade and were preparing to make an example of him.

Contacting Harrison, he explained the situation and asked if he would be willing to take Josh on at his ranch in Texas. If so, his son was not to be afforded any special consideration. He was to be treated as just another hired hand. It was time he learned the meaning of responsibility. Without hesitation, Harrison had wired him back immediately. His son was more than welcome. A little rebellious at first, the young man eventually settled in and applied himself at learning all there was to know about working a Texas cattle ranch. He worked harder than any two cowboys, and soon gained the respect of the men and the general in particular.

When a rampaging longhorn killed the Circle H foreman earlier in the year, Harrison had gone to the older hands, many of whom had served with him in the war, and asked if they would be offended if he gave the job to thirty-year-old Josh. Out of respect for the general and Josh's father, and the fact that the man had proved himself to be a top hand, there were no objections. His little escapade at The Bull's Head the other night had been the first time in four years Harrison had ever known Josh to be drunk. But that was understandable to the man. No one had been working harder to put an end to this rustling than Josh Kincade. Failure was not something the man accepted easily.

Harrison leaned forward. Tossing the butt of his cigar out into the yard, he said, "And that's how it all come about, Mister Law. Josh is a man. He's earned everything he's got, just as his father wanted. He comes from good stock, and the men respect him. Don't guess a man can ask for more than that."

J.T. agreed. "You're right, sir. Especially that part about coming from good stock. One look at Lucy is sure enough proof of that."

Harrison laughed as he stood and stretched. "Oh, to be twenty-five years younger. I better get on to bed. I appreciate you forgoing your sleep to listen to an old man ramble on, Mister Law. Thank you."

J.T. stood as he replied, "I enjoyed it, sir. Never had better company. Goodnight."

Harrison patted the bounty man's shoulder as he walked by.

"I'm glad you are here. Goodnight, son."

Once the general went inside, J.T. sat back down on the swing. It was clear to him that although Harrison didn't openly show it, he was worried about Josh. Given the young foreman's determination and temperament it was only a matter of time before he and some of the boys from the ranch were going to meet somewhere out there on the vast expanses of Texas prairie. When they did, people were going to die. It was Harrison's fear that Josh would be one of those left facedown in the Texas dirt when it was all over. J.T. could only hope that he would be riding at Josh's side when that time came.

TEN

✶

FRANK BOYD HAD been taught well by Deke Toban. Halting his crew at the edge of town, he singled out Choctaw Jones and Quincy Cole to ride into town with him. Six strangers riding in a group could draw unwanted attention. Boyd told the other three men to wait fifteen minutes then follow. They would all meet up at The Bull's Head saloon and decide a course of action once he had talked to Joe Wright.

Crossing the suspension bridge, Boyd headed straight for the sheriff's office. Jones and Cole waited in the saddle while their leader went inside. A few minutes later he came out. The sheriff wasn't there. A deputy told him Wright was more than likely still having breakfast at The Ambrose Hotel. The trio ambled down the street toward the hotel. Heck Ramsey came out of his office when he noticed the three men passing. One of the men, the rider on the outside, looked familiar. He'd seen the face somewhere before but couldn't fix a name to the fellow—not just yet, anyway.

Remaining a respectable distance behind the riders, the marshal strolled along the boardwalk, following the trio. He was curious to see where they were going. An experienced lawman who was known for his uncanny attention to detail, Ramsey's mind sorted through the countless pictures and descriptions of wanted men, posters he viewed each and every day. With each step he took he was certain he had seen one on the man he was following.

The trio stopped in front of The Ambrose Hotel. Ramsey quickly stepped into a hardware store and observed their movements through the window. One of the men stepped down from his horse just as Joe Wright came walking out the door of the hotel, working a toothpick between his teeth. When he looked up and saw the man and his two friends, Ramsey thought the sheriff was going to have a heart attack on the spot. Even from across the street, the marshal could see the color drain from the man's face.

Wright's head snapped left then right to see who, if anyone, might be watching. The big fellow with the beard who had climbed down from his horse stepped up onto the boardwalk. The two talked for moment, all the while Wright's head working as if it were on a swivel. Grabbing the man by the arm, the sheriff pulled him into the hotel lobby. Ramsey couldn't tell what they were talking about, but it was obvious that Wright was more than a little upset about this unexpected meeting on the street. The two went farther into the hotel and Ramsey lost sight of them. A few moments later the big man came out and gave some orders to his two companions, who nodded then headed their horses back down the street, reining in at The Bull's Head saloon. The big fellow then went back into the hotel. Ramsey waited at the window for awhile, but there was no sight of Wright and his visitor. Hurrying back to his office, Ramsey was about to go inside when he noticed three more tough-looking strangers walk their horses by and tie up at The Bull's Head. He shouted inside for his deputy.

"Rich, come out here."

The deputy stepped to the door. "Yeah, Marshal. What's going on?"

"I ain't sure, but every damn hair on the back of my neck tells me it ain't good. Look at them fellows dismountin' in front of The Bull's Head. You recognize any of 'em?"

The deputy studied them for a few seconds. "Can't say I do, Heck. But . . ."

The man stopped in mid-sentence as Jones and Cole came out of the saloon and began talking with the new arrivals.

"Damn! I know that one fellow. The Indian-lookin' one. That's Choctaw Jones. One mean sonofabitch. Watched him gut a fellow in a fight down along the border last summer. Folks say he's pretty good with that gun of his, too."

"How about that other fellow with him?" asked Ramsey, referring to Quincy Cole.

"Can't say. But by the way he wears that iron tied down, I'd say he uses it for more than shootin' snakes. Matter of fact, all them fellows look like a pretty rough bunch. What'd you figure they're doin' in Waco?"

Ramsey shook his head. "Don't know. But the leader of the outfit is meetin' with our county sheriff right now."

The deputy didn't bat an eye as he said, "Looks like John Thomas Law might be right about our sheriff."

Ramsey gave his deputy a hard look. "Talkin' to somebody isn't proof, Rich. But I got to admit, this don't look good. I want you to keep an eye on those boys in the saloon but don't bother 'em none. I need to check somethin' out."

Rich grabbed his hat off the rack inside the door and headed across the street to do as he was told, while Ramsey went to his desk and began sorting through the posters. If nothing else, there might be some paper on this man called Choctaw Jones. A man with a reputation as mean as Rich said had to be wanted by the law somewhere.

JOE WRIGHT SLAMMED the door to the back room of his office shut and turned on Frank Boyd. The sheriff's eyes blazed with anger and his face was turning red as he spoke.

"What the hell is wrong with you boys! Jesus Christ, men, practically everybody in this damn county is looking for cattle rustlers and train robbers. Strangers draw attention around here faster than flies on a shit pile, an y'all come ridin' down the goddamn street bold as brass. Then ya come right straight to me! Don't ya think some people mighta took notice of that? Goddamnit, what was Corbin thinkin' sendin' ya here? Hell, I just sent that telegram last night warnin' him we could have big trouble."

Boyd waited until the man finished, then snapped, "Look you little sonofabitch, the only damn wire I know about is the one you sent about Buck Toban bein' shot dead. I don't know nothin' about no telegram bein' sent last night. We left the ranch two days ago. The Cap'n sent us here to get the bastard who killed Buck and take him back to the ranch. Hell, Deke don't even know his brother's dead. If he did, you'd have nearly fifty men tearin' this damn town apart right now. So quit your bitchin' and tell me where we can find the man who shot Buck an' we'll be getting out of here."

Wright plopped his fat butt on a corner of the desk and stared at Boyd.

"How many men did ya bring with ya?" he asked.

"Five—six, countin' me. Why?"

"I ain't so sure that's enough for what ya boys got in mind."

Boyd was quickly becoming impatient with this man. "What the hell are talkin' about now, Wright?"

"Ya know who shoot them two friends of yer's?"

"Hell, if I knew that I wouldn't be wastin' my time dancin' around here with you, now would I, you dumb bastard."

A grin suddenly came over Wright's face as he said, "Well, we'll just see who the dumb bastard is. The man Corbin sent you for is John Thomas Law."

Boyd had to admit the little man sure knew how to take the air out of a fellow.

"J.T. Law—the bounty man?"

It was all Wright could do to keep from laughing out loud as he had watched Boyd's face lose some color at hearing the name.

"That's the fellow. He's the one who killed Buck. Kline and Buck tried to bushwhack Doc Holliday comin' out of a saloon. Doc killed Kline, and Law gunned Buck. I'd say ya boys mighta bit off mor'n ya could chew on this one."

Boyd wanted to reach out and slap that stupid grin off the fat man's face, but that wouldn't solve anything.

"Is Doc Holliday with Law?"

"Nope. Doc left town already. I think he was headin' for Fort Griffin."

"That's good. That makes it six against one. What about Law? Do you know where he went?"

Wright stood up and walked over to a map of the county he had hanging on the wall and pointed to the section that identified the Circle H Ranch. "The man ya want is stayin' right here. The Circle H. But then you boys are familiar with that, ain't ya? Ya were just out that way a week or so ago if I remember right. Now, how yer gonna get yer hands on him while he's there, I got no idea. Harrison's got close to thirty men workin' for him out there. If he thinks enough of J.T. Law to have him stay at his house, I doubt he's gonna let the six of ya just ride in there and haul him off without a fight."

Boyd studied the map for minute than asked, "What kind of horse is Law ridin'?"

"Big buckskin. Damn good-lookin' animal. Ya can't miss him."

"Okay. Now what's this business about a wire you sent to the cap'n last night?" asked Boyd.

Wright went on to explain about Law somehow coming up with the name "Captain Jack" and sending the telegram to the Texas Rangers in Austin wanting information on Kline and Buck. Once Deke was linked to his brother there was a good chance that all of this could lead J.T. Law to search for Deke and ultimately lead him straight to Captain Jack Corbin.

"So really, the only person askin' all the questions an' causin' us any problem is John T. Law. We get rid of him an' everybody's happy, right? So what's the problem?"

Wright shook his head. "Well, if ya don't consider a gunman like J.T. Law a problem, friend, yer either awful damn good with that there gun or yer a walkin' dead man with big ambitions."

"I'm both. The only dead man is going to be that damn bounty hunter. You wire the cap'n that everything is going

to be taken care of and not to worry about nothin'. You think
you can do that without bitchin'?"

"Sure. I'll send it right away," said Wright.

Boyd left through the back way and went to The Bull's
Head. He found his crew at a table near the end of the bar.
He pulled up a chair and poured himself a drink as Breed
asked, "You find out where our man is?"

"Oh, yeah. A place about seven or eight miles south of
here," said Boyd, as he downed the drink in one smooth
action, then poured himself another.

Jones and Cole had been around Boyd long enough to
know when something was wearing on the man. "What's
wrong, Frank?" asked Quincy.

"Nothin' really. Just a couple of changes to the plan, that's
all. The man we want is stayin' at the Circle H. No way we
can get our hands on him there. We're goin' to have to watch
the place an' wait until he gets clear of the ranch before we
try anything."

"You said a couple of things, my friend. What's the other
change?" asked Breed.

Boyd looked across the table at Jones as he replied, "We
kill him first chance we get."

Quincy seemed surprised. "I thought we were suppose to
take him back so Deke could do that. He ain't gonna like
that, Frank. I think we better stick with the plan of grabbin'
the fellow and takin' him back. That's what the captain
wanted."

"Yeah, well, Deke and the cap'n ain't here, are they."

Breed looked deep into Boyd's eyes. Sitting back in his
chair he said, "Something's wrong Frank. You're scared. I
can see it in your eyes. What is it?"

All eyes at the table were on Boyd as the men waited for
a challenge to Breed for his remark, or an answer from their
leader.

"The man who killed Buck was John Thomas Law."

"Jesus!" uttered Quincy, as he slumped back in his chair.
"The bounty man, himself."

Breed lowered his head and rubbed at his eyes. When he
looked again he replied, "You're right about one thing,

Frank. He sure as hell won't let us get close enough to grab him. We're gonna have to kill him."

"And from a distance, too," said another man at the table. "They say the damn man can shoot the eyes out of a snake's head at thirty yards. I'd say this is more of a job for long guns, not pistols."

Another of the men downed his drink then said, "All of a sudden five hundred dollars don't seem like much for goin' up against J.T. Law. No, sir. It surely don't."

This angered Frank at first, but then the man had only said what he was sure the others were thinking. Fearing that some of them might back out and knowing he would need every gun at that table, Frank on his own raised the bonus money to $1,000 a man. After having received Wright's telegram, Boyd was certain the captain wouldn't mind paying the price.

"When do we head out?" asked Quincy Cole.

"Right now," said Boyd.

Finishing off their drinks, the men stood and headed for the door. As they came up alongside Rich, who was standing at the bar, Breed stopped and said, "Hey, Frank. We're gonna need some supplies."

The man had a point. They could be in the hills watching the ranch for days before they got their chance at John T. Law. They'd need food and coffee. Pulling some money from his shirt pocket, Frank passed it to Breed, telling him to get what they needed and to meet them on the other side of the bridge in an hour.

"What time is it now?" asked Breed.

Rich, trying hard to seem as though he was just another cowboy at the bar, watched in the mirror as Boyd pulled a gold watch from his vest and clicked it open. Giving the time, he was about to put it away when Quincy made a remark about the picture of the young woman inside and asked what her name was. "Sara," proclaimed Boyd with a laugh, "whoever that is."

Rich never turned around, keeping his eyes on the mirror he watched Boyd click the watch closed. It was then that the deputy noticed for the first time the scar across the bridge of Frank Boyd's nose. The lawman felt his stomach tighten. He

wanted to turn and run straight to Ramsey's office and tell
him the news, but he had to wait. Any sudden moves now
could be fatal. For the deputy it seemed as through it took
the men forever to get to the doors and finally leave. Downing his drink, Rich calmly walked out of the saloon and down
the street to the marshal's office. Once inside, he couldn't
contain his excitement.

"It's them, Marshal! It's them!"

Ramsey jumped to his feet. "What in the blue blazes are
you talkin' about, Rich?'

"It's the men who robbed the train!"

"Where?"

"In the saloon! Or, no . . . they were in the saloon, but now
they're gone—or some of 'em are gone. But it's them!
There's the watch . . . and the nose . . . yes, the nose—the
scar—it's there. I saw it."

Ramsey grabbed the man by the arms and forced him
down in a chair. He had to calm him down; none of what
he was saying was making any sense. Pouring a glass of
whiskey from the bottle in his desk, the marshal pushed it
into Rich's hand and told him to take a long drink. When he
had finished Ramsey said, "Okay, now, Rich. Slow and easy.
Start from the beginning. You're talking about the men I sent
you to watch in the saloon, is that right?"

With his heart rate returning to normal, the deputy was
more coherent now.

"Yes, sir. Did like you said. I stayed far enough away that
they didn't really notice me. I couldn't hear anything they
were talking about, but when they were leaving they were
standing right behind me. One of the men said they needed
to get some supplies because they might have to be staying
in the hills for a few days. Then this big man, the one with
the beard, he pulled out a gold watch. There was a picture
of a young woman named Sara inside—they joked about
that. The man with the watch, he had a real bad-looking scar
across his nose. Remember what J.T. Law said; they stole
his gold watch with a picture of a young woman inside. The
man who took it had a beard and a scar across his nose. You
remember that, don't you, Marshal? Well, this is the watch

and that's the man—I'm sure of it. That means they had to be the ones who robbed the train, right?"

Ramsey couldn't believe that after all the posses and searches that had been looking for months, for members of the gang that had been terrorizing McLennan County, six of them were suddenly roaming about his town. Perhaps it was all coincidence? No, that couldn't be it. The details Rich had just laid out left little doubt in his mind that they were the men that J.T. Law was looking for, especially the big man with the scar.

"What're you gonna do, Marshal?" asked Rich, barely able to contain his excitement.

"Where did you say they were right now?"

"The Indian should be at the general store buyin' up provisions. One mighta stayed to help him—I don't know. But the rest of 'em are supposed to meet him across the bridge in an hour."

Ramsey was already regretting his decision to make John T. Law leave town. Bounty man or not, his ability with a Colt would be welcome right now. Ramsey knew he was in a bad fix; two of his best deputies had left at dawn this morning to escort the prison wagon to Austin. That just left Rich, and given his level of excitement Ramsey wasn't sure just how helpful the young man would be in a gun battle. Especially going up against six men that were as tough-looking a bunch as Ramsey had seen in a long time.

Ramsey pulled two shotguns off the rack. He tossed one to Rich along with a box of shells.

"Hightail it over to the court house. Tell the judge what's going on. Tell him I'm gonna need some help from some of his vigilantes."

Rich looked startled. "You mean the judge knows who's in the vigilantes?"

"Hell, kid, everybody in this town's got some dirty little secret. He'll deny he knows any of that bunch, but you tell him I know different and to get us some help. Now go on. I'll be at the general store."

Clutching his shotgun and box of shells, Rich hurried to the door. He suddenly stopped, turned, and watching Ramsey break open his scatter gun and load two shells, he said, "Heck—you be careful. Like I said, that Choctaw Jones is a bad one."

"You just get movin', boy. I can take care of myself."

Cradling the scatter gun, Ramsey walked out of his office and headed for the general store. Through the store front window he saw Choctaw Jones standing at the counter talking with the clerk. Cocking the hammers back on the double-barrel, he leveled the gun and stepped inside. The clerk's eyes went big as saucers. Seeing this, Breed whirled around, his hand dropping to his holster.

"Don't do it, Jones—you got no chance!" shouted Ramsey.

Even facing a double-barrel shotgun, Ramsey could tell the man was thinking about pulling on him. There was no fear in his face.

"Now you just reach over with that left hand and unhitch that gunbelt and let it drop, you hear me," said Ramsey in a cold, hard tone. "You don't, I'm gonna cut you in half where you stand. Your choice."

Breed slowly did as he was told. The marshal motioned toward the door. Telling the clerk to pick up the gun belt and bring it to him, Ramsey told Breed, "Okay, let's go. We're goin' to my office. You stay in front of me and don't do nothin' foolish."

People quickly cleared the boardwalk as the two men made their way toward the marshal's office. A small group of curious onlookers followed along behind them. Across the street, someone paused at the doorway to Wright's office and shouted, "Hey, Sheriff, you got any idea what's goin' on out here?"

Joe Wright moved to the doorway and stared out. He felt his heart skip a couple of beats. "Dammit!" he uttered under his breath. He recognized Jones as being one of the men who had been with Frank Boyd. This wasn't good. He doubted the man would talk, but the fact that Ramsey had him was cause enough to be concerned.

Returning to his desk, Wright was trying to figure out what to do when Jenkins came in. He had a telegram in his hand.

"Got a reply to that message you sent last night," he said, as he handed the paper to Wright.

It was from Corbin and read:

"TELL FB CHANGE OF PLAN STOP HANDLE SITUATION ON HIS OWN STOP NO NEED TO BRING PACKAGE HERE STOP END IT THERE STOP EXPECT YOU TO LEND AS-SISTANCE AS NEEDED STOP WILL BE IN WACO IN TWO DAYS STOP KEEP ME INFORMED STOP"

Wright crumpled the paper in his hand. "This damn thing's startin' to get out of hand an' it's all that damn bounty hunter's doin'."

"What're you gonna do?" asked Jenkins.

Wright tossed the telegram to the man. "I want ya to take that to Frank Boyd. You'll find him and his men waiting across the bridge. He's a big fellow with a beard and a scar across his nose. Ya tell him I said to get his business done out at the H. I'll take care of getting his man outta jail. I want this bunch out of my county as soon as they done dealt with that damn bounty hunter. Ya tell him that. Now go on."

Jenkins started to protest but quickly changed his mind when he saw the threatening look on Wright's face. "Okay, but I don't want no part of any gun play, Joe. I'm just a wire operator an' delivery man, that's all."

"Just get yer ass on across that bridge an' do what I told ya."

As Jenkins closed the door behind him, Wright set down at his desk. He had to figure out how he was going to get that man out of Heck Ramsey's jail. One thing for sure—it wasn't going to be easy.

ELEVEN

AFTER BREAKFAST, JOHN T. told Josh he wanted to meet with some of the ranchers who had been hit by the rustlers. Maybe by working together they could come up with a plan to lure the gang out in the open and into a trap. Josh asked how many men he should bring along.

"Three should be enough—just make sure that Jed Davis is one of them."

The gunfighter saw the concerned look that came over the young ramrod's face.

"Don't worry, Josh. I know what I'm doin'."

While J.T. saddled Toby, Josh disappeared into the bunk-house. When he came back out he had three men with him; Jed Davis was in the lead. While the group readied their horses, Davis looked over his saddle at J.T.

"Takin' a hell of a chance ain't you, bounty hunter? I just might find it hard to keep my promise to young Josh once we get out there on the prairie. Be a damn good time to settle up accounts."

John T. tightened the cinch on Toby and with a devil-may-care grin gave Davis something to think about.

"I'm countin' on you doin' just that, Mister Davis."

With the group saddled and ready to ride, Josh led out with J.T. close behind, allowing Davis a clear shot at his back if the man had a mind to take it. But J.T. didn't figure the man would. He didn't have the look or manner of a backshooter and the fact that he had been with the general since the war, if he pulled such a low-down trick, he was sure to lose the respect of his longtime friend and commander.

The first ranch they headed for was the Bar B owned by Big Mike Brown, an early pioneer in Texas. Having staked out his land, he'd fought Indians, Comancheros and Mexican bandits to hold on to it. It was a ranch that had been paid for in blood. As they rode through the gate, Josh nodded toward a white picket fence that surrounded a cemetery. There were two fresh mounds of dirt near the front. One of those graves was Brown's eldest son, who had been killed by the rustlers only a few weeks earlier.

As they approached the house, Mike Brown came out onto the porch to greet them. He was a tall man; not big and wide, but rather, long and wiry. He had salt-and-pepper hair that matched a full beard. The face was wrinkled and lined, showing years of hard work and exposure to a harsh land. He greeted Josh as they walked their horses up to the front porch.

"Howdy, Josh. What's brings you boys this far south? Them damn outlaws hit you all again?"

"No, nothin' like that, Mike." Pointing to J.T., Josh said, "This here is John T. Law; he's spendin' a little time out at our place. He's got an interest in findin' the bunch that's been causing all the trouble around here."

Brown knew the name well. "I'll just bet he does. Bounty hunter could make himself a pretty good payday closin' down that bunch. I heard of you, Law. They say you're damn good with that iron, but you're still just one man. There's got be near on to thirty or more of them fellows in that outfit. That's a mighty big job, even for a man like you."

"You're right, Mister Brown. That's why we're here," said J.T. "No one man alone can bring these boys down. It's gonna take all the ranchers workin' together. If you got a little time, maybe we could talk about that."

Slapping his leg hard, Brown shook his head. "Damn. Where the hell are my manners? Of course. You fellows step on down and come in the house. I'll have my woman fix us some coffee or lemonade if you want." Turning around, Brown yelled into the house. "Hey, Mattie! We got company."

Brown sent for his foreman. The group sat around talking about the raids and the different methods the ranchers were using to try and stop any further loss of their cattle. When J.T. asked about the night the Bar B had been hit, the foreman told him he had been a cavalryman in the war and the method of attack used by the rustlers were almost textbook cavalry tactics right down to having a rear guard in place to discourage anyone who went after them. Mike Brown's son and another cowboy had died in the ambush while chasing the rustlers.

It was exactly the kind of answer J.T. had expected. His theory wasn't just a theory anymore; this proved he was right. Whoever was running this operation had prior military experience and it was a good bet the man had been a cavalry officer.

J.T. told Brown that he thought if they could put together a herd so big that people would begin talking about it, then let it slip that they were driving the cattle to Mexico for sale to the Mexican government, maybe, just maybe, it would be too big a prize for the gang to resist. When they made their move, the ranchers and Abe Covington's Texas Rangers would be waiting for them and spring the trap. At least it was worth a try.

Brown didn't hesitate to agree. He would talk to the other ranchers. Knowing the way they felt, he was certain that they would want to be in on the kill, even if it cost them a few more cows. All the owners could meet at the general's ranch tomorrow night, if that was all right. Josh assured Brown that it would be fine with Harrison. As a matter of fact, the general had some friends from the capitol coming for a visit. It would be a good time to give the politicians an idea of what was going on. Their business finished, Josh and J.T. thanked Brown for his hospitality. Telling the man they would see him tomorrow night, they bid him farewell and rode away.

"That's a pretty slick idea you had back there, John T. You must have put a lot of thought into it. When did you come up with it?"

Law smiled. "While we were riding over here."

"Just come to you like that—outta the blue, huh?"

"Not really. I had a friend who used to ride with Jesse James. Only time Jesse come close to bein' caught was when he got greedy. The Pinkertons fooled him into believin' that there was a special train loaded with gold coins headed from the Denver Mint to Kansas City. It was some ungodly amount of money, I don't remember . . . or, I mean, my friend didn't remember how much it was—but it was plenty. Anyway, they got the schedule for the train and hit it outside Kansas City. There wasn't no gold, but three boxcars full of federal marshals, Pinkertons, and even a few army troops. Jesse lost four good men that night, not to the lawmen on the train, but to a posse that was out looking for them for a bank job they had just pulled three days earlier. You see, Jesse had broke his own rule. And that rule was that you always laid low for four or five weeks after a robbery."

Josh's eyes were big as he listened to J.T. tell the story; after all, this was Jesse James the man was talking about. "Why would he do that, John T.?"

"Because posses are made up mostly of townspeople. They're all excited and ready to go at first, but after a week in the saddle, eatin' out of a can and sleepin' on the ground, the excitement's pretty much gone and those towns folk want to get back to their warm houses and soft beds. But until then, they're always a threat to stumble onto a gang unexpected like. Jesse was so blinded by the thought of all that gold that he forgot about that. Nearly got him killed, too. We . . . uh . . . I mean, they were ridin' so hard to get away from the Pinkertons that they rode blind straight into a forty-man posse coming the other way. By the time the shootin' was over, four of the James Gang were dead and two wounded."

"I'll be damned. So you think these boys we're after are kind of like the James Boys. Using hit-and-run tactics, right?" asked Josh.

"That's right, Josh. Whoever is runnin' the show for this gang is pretty much doing the same thing as Jesse. They hit a place then disappear for two or three weeks, then come right back and hit another one, then disappear again for awhile until things cool down and the posses have given up on findin' anything and head home. They hit your ranch a week ago. The Brown place three weeks earlier. If they stick to the routine, they won't be out raidin' again for two or three more weeks. Like the Pinkertons, I'm hopin' we can put together a big enough prize that they'll break their routine and greed will take over. That happens—we got 'em."

They rode along at a casual pace for a ways then Josh asked, "You said Jesse got the schedule for that special train—how'd he do that?"

J.T. pulled back on the reins, bringing Toby to a stop.

Josh halted beside him. "What's wrong, J.T.?"

"Damn! I must be getting old, Josh."

"What'd you mean?"

"What you just said about the schedule. Jesse used informants. They hung around the bars listenin' for any news about gold shipments goin' out or comin' in on stages or trains. But his main source of information came from telegraph operators he was able to bribe. That's how this gang knew which trains were carrying gold the other day. The telegraph operator. He must be on the outlaws' payroll."

"Jenkins!" said, Josh. "I find that hard to believe, J.T. The man walks around scared of his own shadow. Wouldn't figure him to be hooked with a rough bunch like this."

"Don't kid yourself, Josh. Enough money can make even a coward take risks. And if I'm right about that sheriff of yours, it's almost sure they're both workin' together. I think we better go in an' have a talk with this Jenkins fellow in the morning."

• • •

COMING UP TO a creek, J.T. stopped the group for a rest and to give the horses a chance to drink. Pulling a slim cigar from his leather vest, J.T. walked over to a tree and was about to light up when Jed Davis shouted, "Turn around, Law!"

Josh jumped to his feet. "Goddamnit, Jed, you gave me your word! Now you back down right now, You hear?"

J.T. stood perfectly still, his back to Davis. "Stay out of this, Josh. That goes for you other boys, too. This ain't your fight."

"Sorry, Josh," said Jed. "Ain't never broke my word to you before, but this is different. This man killed a good friend of mine. Shot him down like a dog, an' for nothin' but my friend's share of some damn reward money. Ain't that right, bounty man? You killed your own partner, didn't you, John Law?"

John T. felt his body tense. Now it all made sense to him. The incident suddenly flashed before his eyes. It had been a nightmare that had taken years to put behind him but now here it was seven years later and it was back. But Jed Davis had the story all wrong. Raising his hands, J.T. slowly turned around to face his adversary. Davis already had his gun drawn, the hammer back. Josh and the other two cowhands had moved back toward the creek out of the line of fire.

"So you were a friend of Billy Claymont." said Law.

Davis's face was tense and drawn, the eyes fired by vengeance. "You don't deny he was your partner when you started out in the bounty business, do you?"

"No, I don't. Me and Billy met down in Brownsville. He was as down on his luck as I was at the time. We only had enough money to buy two damn drinks, but that was plenty. We talked awhile. Seemed like we had a lot in common. Next thing you know, we set out in the bounty business together. Figured that way we could watch each other's back. Didn't make much when we first started out, but the longer we worked at it the better we got. Before long we were bringing in some fair-size money. But it was never enough. Billy had a thing for the whores, but then I reckon you already knew."

Davis nodded, "Yeah, that's right. I knew his pa, an' watched the kid grow up. Billy loved the ladies, sure enough. Saw him in Dallas, summer of seventy. Told me he'd hooked up with you and was gonna make a fortune as a bounty man. Gonna bump every whore in Texas at least once 'fore he was through. Hell, three weeks later he was dead—an' it was you that killed him—his own damn partner,"

"That's right, I sure as hell did. Since you seem to know so much about it, why don't you tell Josh and the boys why I killed the sonofabitch," said Law without a sign of fear showing on his face.

"Jesus, J.T.," said, Josh, as he watched Davis's face go crimson and his finger tighten on the trigger. "Come on, Jed. Tell us why this man killed your friend."

Davis seemed to relax for a moment as he answered, "They caught up to a pair of outlaws who had killed a judge over in Fort Worth. The law had put up five thousand and the family another ten thousand for both men, dead or alive. They killed one and damn near walked the other one to death pullin' him along on rope behind a horse. Couple of days later they got their money and were doin' the town. Sometime after midnight there was shootin' coming from Billy's room. John T. Law here had killed Billy for his share of the reward money. They found it scattered all over the floor of the room. The news almost caused the death of that boy's folks, but I swore I'd get even for 'em one day and here we are. Hell, you heard him. He don't even deny he killed him."

"How about it, John T.?" asked Josh. "Is that the story?"

"Oh, I killed him all right. But Mister Davis here has his story a little backward. I went to take a bath that night. When I come back to the room, I found my money was gone. First I thought somebody had robbed me an' that they would be going after Billy next. I took my gun and went to his room, half expectin' to find him out cold or worse. I busted into the room and there was Billy with two whores. They were all buck naked and rollin' back an' forth in the money that was spread all over the bed. When I asked him what the hell he was doin' with my money, he just laughed. It pissed me off at the time. I went to the bed, shoved the whores off the money and counted out what I figured was mine. Told Billy if he wanted to drink until he passed out an' lost his damn money, that was his business. I was going to put mine in the hotel safe downstairs."

J.T. paused for moment, the memory of what happened next still painful to remember. "When I reached for the door, I heard a shot and felt hot lead slam into my back. Before I could turn around, a second shot hit me just below the left shoulder blade and came out my left side. I managed to turn, and saw Billy on his knees on the bed with his gun in his hand. I don't know why he did what he did. Crazy drunk, maybe. I just don't know. He was about to fire again. The whores were covering their ears and screaming like banshees. I fired one shot. It hit Billy in the heart, killing him. I don't remember much after that. The girls were still screamin' and some more people come runnin' into the room. Money was scattered everywhere. Somebody yelled for the doctor, an' I passed out. I came to three days later; they'd already buried Billy. The law had got the story from the whores and called it self-defense. Of course, all the money but about eight hundred dollars had disappeared. As soon as I was able to ride, they ran me out of town. They were afraid I might start lookin' for the rest of that money. Billy was the only partner I ever had. I've worked alone ever since. Now that's the real story, Mister Davis. It ain't as pretty as yours maybe—but by God, it's the truth."

J.T. suddenly tore open his shirt and turned his back to Davis. He pulled the shirt up over his head to expose his bullet-scarred back, then said, "Since you claim that sonofabitch as a friend, you go ahead and finish what he started. I won't kill a good man over the likes of that bastard. So you do what you feel you have to do."

Davis's hand began to shake as he stared at the two ugly scars on J.T.'s back. He didn't want to believe what he had heard, but he couldn't deny what he saw before his very own eyes. And there was something about the way Law had told the story that rang true. He had told it straightforward and without hesitation. And now this. The gunfighter was offering him his back rather than drawing on him. That wasn't something a lying man would do. Davis looked over at Josh and the other two drovers. It was plain to see they believed the man's story. Neither of them would look Jed in the eye.

He had the gun, it was his decision.

Jed Davis felt like a fool. All these years hating a man for something he would have done himself. Lowering the pistol and shoving it into the holster, he walked to his horse, swung up into the saddle and rode off without saying a word.

J.T. heard the horse leaving and lowered his arms. Tucking his shirt in he watched Jed ride over the crest of a far hill.

"Where do you figure he's going, J.T.? The ranch is back the other way," said Josh.

"I wouldn't worry none, Josh. Sometimes the truth can be as painful as a bullet in the gut and when it hits a man, he needs some time alone to think things over. Jed's a good man. He'll be back at the ranch by tonight."

One of the drovers brought J.T. his horse. "Here you go, Mister Law," said the cowboy, with an expression of respect on his face.

"Thanks. We ready to ride?"

"Yeah. We best be movin'. We're still an hour from the ranch," answered Josh.

As the men made their way through the valley and down to the flatlands their eyes would occasionally search the hills around them for any sign of Jed Davis. J.T. had just moved up beside Josh when the crack of a rifle echoed and a bullet took the hat off his head.

"Break for the trees!" shouted J.T. as he spurred Toby. The big buckskin leaped forward and broke into full stride. Bullets seem to be coming from everywhere now as the roar of what sounded like four or five rifles echoed across the flatlands. Lead kicked up the dirt all around the riders as they closed in on the timberline and some hope of cover.

J.T. heard the familiar *thud* as a bullet found its mark. He knew someone had been hit. As he looked back, he saw Josh tumble out of the saddle and land hard on the ground. He wasn't moving. One of the drovers pulled up next to the foreman, but before he could help his boss the rifles zeroed in on him. J.T. heard the sickening *thud*s and saw dust fly from the cowboy's shirt as three bullets knocked him out of the saddle. The man was dead before he hit the ground.

The other cowboy had made the woods. Pulling his rifle from the boot he dropped down behind a tree and began to fire at the trees that ran along the ledge of a cliff two hundred yards away and to the left. Reining Toby around, John T. hung over the side of his horse and rode back to where Josh was down. The man still hadn't moved. J.T. was afraid he was dead. With lead kicking up around Toby, J.T. dropped off the horse and rolled Josh over. Blood covered the left side of the man's shirt. He was still breathing, but the breaths were coming in short, rattling gasps. There was blood coming from the corner of his mouth. A small trickle was visible from the right side of his nose.

Ignoring the beehive of lead that was flying all around him, J.T. picked the man up and placed him over his saddle. Swinging up behind him, Law gave Toby a kick and they raced for the trees. Law knew the bouncing around wasn't good for the type of wound Josh had, but leaving him out there in the open, he would have been dead for sure.

Toby broke through the underbrush and into the woods. J.T. pulled Josh from the saddle and laid him on the ground. Ripping his shirt open, Law found what he had expected to find. Josh had taken a round through the back, which had come out his chest. From the labored breathing and wheezing he heard, he knew the bullet had punctured a lung. Grabbing his saddlebags, J.T. dumped the contents on the ground. Ripping a shirt into strips, he set them aside and grabbed an old letter, folding it over. Pouring water from a bag onto the ground, he quickly mixed the dirt and water until he had pile of mud. Placing the paper over the wound he scooped up a handful of the mud and placed it on top of the paper, spreading it out until he had formed an airtight seal. Moving Josh to a sitting position, he wrapped the strips tight around his chest six times and tied it off. Laying him back down, he listened. The breathing had eased some and the rattle sound had all but vanished, but this was only a quick fix. He was going to die if they didn't get him out of there and back to the ranch, and fast.

Grabbing a box of shells from the pile of items next to the saddlebags, J.T. pulled his Winchester rifle from the saddle boot and joined the cowboy firing at the hill. As he dropped down beside the young drover, two bullets skinned the bark off the tree only inches above J.T.'s head.

"Can you see 'em?" asked Law.

"Catch sight of 'em movin' around every now an' then. They don't stay in one spot very long. Fire a couple shots, then move to another position. Don't think I've hit any of 'em yet. How's the boss doin?"

"Not good. Got to get him back to the ranch or he's gonna die out here. You're goin' have to take him."

"But what about you?"

"I'll keep these bastards busy while you get away. Put Josh up on my horse and tie him in. Then you lead him out. Make for the ranch as fast as you can. That boy don't get some proper help in the next couple of hours, he's as good as dead. Think you can handle it?"

The young drover looked back at Josh then to John T. "Hell, yes, I can. But there's only two horses. What about you? There's at least four guns up there, maybe five. I take both those horses you're left afoot. You'll be in a bad way if they decide to ride down on you."

"You let me worry about that, cowboy. Get Josh rigged up and get outta here. You get to the ranch, you can send some help back. Now get movin'. Every minute you waste here is a minute less Josh has to live. Go on!"

The cowboy wished J.T. luck and ran back to the horses. Within minutes he had Josh rigged on Toby and mounted up. Looking back at Law, he waved, then kicked his mount, and holding tight to Toby's reins, headed out through the woods and over the hill for the Circle H, which was still miles away.

Bullets cracked through the trees overhead and kicked up the dirt around J.T.'s position. He would return fire every now and then, but the cowboy was right—they were hard targets to spot. After about five minutes the firing stopped. Reloading his rifle he kept his eyes on the cliff. He was sure they had seen the cowboy haul Josh away on his buckskin and they knew they were only up against one man now and he was afoot.

As the seconds turned into minutes, J.T. tried to figure out just who it was that had ambushed them. His first thought was Joe Wright, but the more he thought about it, the man didn't have enough sand to risk something like this. Then who? Then it came to him. The telegram he'd sent to Covington in Austin. If the operator was working with the rustlers he could have let them know that J.T. was asking a lot of questions and was about to stir up trouble. That had to be it. At least this proved one thing—he must be asking the right questions.

Suddenly there was a flurry of movement among the trees near the cliff. Three riders broke from the woods and rode hell-bent for leather toward the far end of the hill, which had a gradual slope that lead into the trees off to J.T.'s right. They were going to get behind him, then flank him. It was a sound military move. Without a horse, how far was he going to get?

"Damn," said J.T., "got myself in a fine mess this time." Just then, out of the corner of his left eye, there was movement. He swung the rifle in that direction. It was a horse. The chestnut bay that belonged to the dead cowboy who had tried to help Josh. It was wandering about less than thirty yards away. If he could make it to that horse, he had a chance. But as soon as he moved ten feet from the tree a hail of bullets rained down on him from the cliff, forcing him to dive behind a log for cover. Lead tore chunks of wood from the log, sending debris spinning into the air and raining down on his head and shoulders. They had him pinned down good—no doubt about that. And it was just a matter of time before those three riders started working their way in on him from behind.

Crawling to the far end of the log, he peered around the end. The horse was chewing at the prairie grass and gradually working its way toward him. J.T. began to whistle and click his tongue in an effort to get the bay to come to him. It seemed to be working. The horse's ears went up. He stared at J.T. for a moment then began to walk toward the log.

Two rifle shots cracked the air and the bay whinnied, then staggered and fell.

This outraged the bounty man. Bringing the rifle up, he fired off five shots in rapid time as he shouted, "Goddamn you all to hell!"

Dropping back down behind the log he shoved five more rounds into the rifle. There were two things that made him madder than hell: the mistreatment of children and horses. He was wishing now he'd scared the bay off rather than calling it to him. From behind the log he heard the sound of horses. Looking over the log, he saw the two riflemen from the cliff heading down the slope to the left and cutting back toward him. Before he could get off a shot, they swung their horses into the tree line. They were closing in on him.

Jumping to his feet, he ran back to his saddlebags. J.T. pulled his short-barrel Colt and the shoulder rig out and put them on. Next came the Bowie knife: a wicked-looking blade, twelve inches long and razor sharp. He eased the blade and scabbard down into his boot. They wanted a war, then fine. He had plenty of experience at that game. He wasn't going to sit and wait for them to come for him. He was going to take the fight to them.

Frank Boyd signaled to Quincy with his hand, motioning for the man to move farther over to his right. Quincy in turn passed the signal on to the man to his right. Slowly, quietly, the men walked their horses toward the small area where they had last seem their prey. They had formed a half-moon circle and were now closing it in around J.T. Law. Any second now they expected to see the man spring from his hole like a trapped march hare and when he did they would cut him down.

The rider at the far end of the semicircle lost sight of Quincy as they moved into thicker trees and scrub. He pulled up and listened intently. For a moment he thought he'd heard something behind him. Moving slow in the saddle so as to make as little noise as possible, the rider turned to look behind him. He could have sworn he heard something, but there was nothing there. As he turned back to the front the man felt a sudden pain in his chest, as if someone had hit him with a club. The blow took the air out of him. Lowering his head he saw the handle of the Bowie knife protruding from his chest. He opened his mouth to scream. But there were no words, only the rusty copper taste of blood, which bubbled from between his lips and down the front of his shirt. The man's eyes rolled back and he tilted sideways, falling out of his saddle.

J.T. quickly ran forward and caught the man as he fell. Pulling his foot from the stirrup, he quietly lowered the body to the ground. Pulling the dead man's six-gun from its holster, he shoved it in his belt, next to his stomach. Next came the knife. These sonofabitches wanted a war, well now they were going to get one, guerrilla style. Swinging up into the saddle, the former raider drew his Colt Peacemaker and giving a high-pitched Rebel yell, slapped spurs to his mount, charging headlong through the woods, weaving his horse right and left, barely missing trees. He bore down on the next man in the line.

The sudden yell had brought Boyd and the others to a stop. The man on the far right of the line looked to his left. It sounded as if a bear were tearing its way through the woods. J.T. suddenly burst into the clearing. The man was so startled to see this wild man bearing down on him that he hesitated in bringing his rifle up. That was a mistake that cost him his life as J.T. fired three rapid shots into the man's chest from less than twenty feet away.

J.T. didn't even bother to watch the man fall. Storming past him, the bounty man bore down on the next fellow, who managed to get off two shots. Both missed their mark when J.T. slid out of the saddle and over to the right side of his horse. With his left boot hooking the seat of the saddle, he leaned forward and snapped off two shots from under the horse's neck. Both hit the man in the head and sent him tumbling backward out of the saddle.

Quincy Cole had watched the action in stunned amazement. "Goddamnest thing I ever saw," he uttered as he watched Law right himself in the saddle and slide the Peacemaker back into the holster, while at the same time drawing the short-barrel Colt from his shoulder rig. "I'll be damned!

That's a Bloody Bill Anderson man if I ever saw one. I know this game, by God!"

Tossing his rifle aside, Quincy drew his pistol. Kicking his horse hard, he broke into a dead run straight at John Law. Both men were firing. J.T.'s first bullet tore through Quincy's leg, but didn't even slow the man down. Law felt his shirt jerk at the collar as Quincy's shot passed an inch from the side of his throat. J.T.'s next shot caught the fearless Quincy square in the chest, the impact knocking him out of the saddle, but not before he got off a shot that struck Law's horse in the head. The animal dropped like a rock, spilling J.T. forward and sending him tumbling end over end until he finally came to rest against a tree stump.

Dazed and half out of it, J.T. saw the last rider coming toward him. He raised his hand, then realized he had lost his Colt when he fell. He grabbed for the belly gun, but it was gone as well. It lay in the dirt fifteen feet away. He started to pull the Peacemaker, but that wouldn't help; he'd fired every round. Still dazed and breathing hard from the pain of a broken rib, the bounty man accepted his fate and leaned back against the stump. He'd given it a good run, but he had come up short.

Frank Boyd walked his horse up to within a few feet of Law and looked down at the man. He held a .45 loosely in his hand. "Gotta admit, Law—I heard people say you were one hard bastard, but after seein' you in action, don't think they done you justice. Cap'n ain't gonna like it, you killin' four of his best boys. But then, long as I show up with your damn head on a stick, guess it won't matter none."

J.T. pulled the stub of a broken cigar out of his shirt pocket and stuck it in the corner of his mouth. It moved up and down as he smiled and looked up at Boyd saying, "Would'd been five if that fellow hadn't shot my horse. But shootin' horses is about all you sonsabitches are good at."

Boyd laughed out loud. "Gotta be a hard-ass to the end, do you? Well, you got class, John Thomas Law, I'll give you that. Too bad. You shoulda kept your nose outta our business."

Now it was Law who laughed. "Looking at that damn

scarred-up nose of yours I'd say you was the one needed that advice. By any chance, you got the time?"

Boyd nodded his head. "You know I do. Hell, I should'a killed you on that damn train when I had the chance. Woulda, too, if I'd know'd who ya was. Figure Quincy and the other boys you killed back in them woods are wishin' I would have, too."

Pulling J.T.'s gold watch from his pocket, Boyd clicked it open. "Damn good-lookin' woman you got here, Law. I like tellin' folks she's my gal. Didn't figure you'd mind." Holding the watch out so Law could see it, Boyd, laughed again, "Well, looky there, bounty man. This here fine gold watch of mine says yer time's run out. Time for ya to die."

Clicking the gold case shut, he slipped it back in his pocket. Cocking the hammer back on the .45, Boyd sat up in the saddle and took aim at John Law's head. The bounty man didn't bother to look up. "No hard feelin's," muttered Boyd as he started to squeeze the trigger.

The sound of the shot caused Law to flinch. His eyes closed for a split second. He expected it to be over quick and painless, but instead, he felt a numbing pain shoot up his leg. Opening his eyes, he saw the heel of his boot was gone. Somehow Boyd had missed him. Looking up at the bearded man, he saw Boyd slumped over in the saddle. A piece of his skull was missing and blood was pooling up in the dirt next to the horse's left front leg. J.T. was trying to figure out what the hell had happened, when Jed Davis came walking his horse out of the tree line, the butt of his Spencer rifle held firmly on his right leg. Stopping next to Boyd's slumped-over body, Davis pulled a foot free from the stirrup, raised it and proceeded to kick Boyd out of the saddle. "Cut that a little too close, I reckon. Did he shoot ya?'

"Ruined a damn good pair of boots. How long you been sittin' over there?" asked Law as he struggled to get to his feet.

Davis slid the rifle into the boot and leaned on his saddle horn. "Oh, a while I suppose. Had to do some thinkin' 'bout what ya said earlier. Decided at the last minute that maybe ya was telling the straight of it about Billy. Figured I owed ya."

The feeling was starting to come back in John Law's leg as he hobbled over to Boyd's body, rolled it over and pulled his gold watch from the man's vest pocket. Holding it tightly in his hand, he looked up at Davis. "I want you to know— if Billy hadn't cocked that gun of his a third time, I wouldn't have shot him. He didn't leave me any choice. I'm sorry it happened."

Davis stared off at the mountains as he wiped his nose with the sleeve of his shirt.

"Liquor and whores killed many a man. Both can cloud a man's mind, I reckon. Cause him to make some bad choices. Nothin' a fellow can do 'bout that. Can you ride?"

Law picked up his Colt and pushed it back into the shoulder rig, then moved to Boyd's horse and pulled himself into the saddle. "They got Josh. He was hit pretty bad. I ain't sure he's gonna make it."

Davis nodded. "Yeah, I know. I come across 'em back a ways. That's how I knew where ya was. He didn't look good. Guess we better ride."

As they turned their horses, Law said, "Thank you, Mister Davis."

The old cowboy spit and spurred his horse as he mumbled, "Welcome."

TWELVE

✦

LUCKILY FOR JOSH Kincade, Waco was a growing city that benefitted by having not just one doctor, but four, two of whom were personal friends of Tom Harrison. So when the word came that help was needed immediately at the Circle H, both doctors hurried to their friend's aid. They were fascinated by the crude method that J.T. had used to seal the wound. His quick thinking had contributed in large part to saving the man's life.

As for Law himself, the doctors agreed that he had suffered a broken rib and severely bruised a number of the others. The only thing they could do was to wrap them tightly to ease the pain. It would take a few weeks for him to recover fully from his injuries, but he would be fine.

Harrison sent a crew out to the ambush site with a wagon to gather up the bodies of the dead men. They were brought back to the ranch, and a rider sent into Waco to fetch Marshal Ramsey. Lucy had been a total wreck ever since Josh had been brought to the house. There had been so much blood and talk that it was a bad wound and that her brother might very well die before morning. It was all more than she could stand.

Harrison had tried to comfort her as best he could, but it wasn't until J.T. arrived, and seeing her so distressed, took her hand and assured her that Josh was going to live, that she finally began to calm down and regain some sense of composure. She had heard the doctor's remark that it had been Law's crude medical work that had saved her brother's life, and she had thanked him repeatedly throughout the afternoon. She had done it so often that J.T. was actually getting embarrassed by the way she was fussing over him.

Just before dark, Heck Ramsey arrived. Harrison and J.T. were on the porch.

"Howdy, Tom, Mister Law," said Ramsey as he stepped down from his horse, tying him off at the hitching rail. "Understand Josh was shot this afternoon. How's he doin?"

The general went down the front steps and shook the marshal's hand as he replied, "Doc says he's gonna make it. He was hit pretty bad. Hadn't been for J.T. here, the boy wouldn't have made it."

Ramsey looked up at Law. "It seems you're a man of many talents, Mister Law."

"I get by, Marshal."

"Your rider here told me Mister Law and a fellow named Davis killed the people who did this, and you had the bodies out here. That right?"

Harrison took the man's arm and they started walking toward the barn.

"That's right, Heck. Five of 'em. J.T. got four and Jed Davis the last one. Thought you oughta have a look at them before we planted their miserable souls," said Harrison.

Grabbing a lantern from a post, J.T. walked up to the wagon. Holding the light high, he threw back the blanket covering the dead men. Ramsey stepped in a little closer for a better look.

"I seen all these fellows in town. There were six of them come ridin' in this morning. That one fellow there is Quincy Cole. Thought I recognized him the minute I saw him, but wasn't sure. Did some checking. He use to ride with Sam Bass. Pretty good man with a gun, they say. But obviously not as talented as our Mister Law, here. Don't know any of these other fellows."

"You said six men, Marshal. You know what happened to that sixth man?" asked J.T.

"Yep. Got him locked up in my jail. Real mean sort of a fellow. A breed, goes by the name of Choctaw Jones. You know him?"

Law shook his head. "No, never met the man, but I've heard of him. They say he's fast with a gun. Killed a few men down along the border. Why'd you arrest him?"

Leaning against the wagon, Ramsey looked at J.T. "That fellow there with half a head and a beard was showin' off your watch in The Bull's Head this morning. One of my men saw it: Rich, he was the kid cleaning the scatter gun the day you come in to talk to me. He remembered you talkin' about that watch. He's a smart boy. He put two and two together. Figured these were the fellows who robbed the Austin train and come told me about it. I was tryin' to get some men together to arrest the whole bunch, but it seems nobody was available, especially if there was going to be gun play. So I arrested this Jones fellow first. Before I could go after the rest, they were gone. Seems they had more important business with you."

J.T. felt Ramsey was holding something back and he thought he knew what it was. "Let me ask you something, Marshal. Did any of these men happen to talk with Joe Wright?"

Ramsey showed a slight grin. He was beginning to gain more respect for this man every time he met him. He wasn't just another fast gun. He was smart, too.

"Matter of fact, the big fellow who had your watch went around town looking for him. Found him, too. Joe didn't seem too happy about it either. I don't know what was said, but they talked for awhile. Now let me ask you this one: Why would six men who had robbed a train and got clean away risk gettin' caught looking for you then try an' kill you?"

"Because I'm getting too close to this man Captain Jack."

"How would he know what you were up to?"

"He's got two sources in Waco. One is Joe Wright. I'm convinced of that now. The other is a fellow named Jenkins, the telegraph operator. He's in it up to his neck. He's the one who gave Captain Jack the schedule for the trains carrying the gold shipments. And I don't think those two are the only ones. I believe the leader of this bunch has bribed other operators and lawman from Dallas to the Mexican border. That's why nobody can ever follow them. The lawmen lead posses off in the wrong direction while the operators send false information and directions to the honest lawmen trying to track them down. This isn't some run-of-the-mill outlaw bunch you're dealin' with here. This outfit's got some mighty big plans. Plans that take plenty of money. Now what those plans are, I haven't figured out yet. But I must be on the right track if someone's worried enough to send six gunmen after me."

This new revelation seemed to shock the marshal. That could explain a lot of things. "I have to agree with you. This business has been goin' on for a year now. Ain't no way they could have got away as many times as they have without help. Guess we need to talk to Jenkins and that fellow I got locked up."

Harrison had been listening with interest as the two men talked. Now he said, "You know, if you figure up how many head of cattle that's been stolen you're lookin' at close to fifteen thousand over the last six months. That's a lot of cattle, even for Mexico. I'll bet you they haven't sold all them cows either. Somewhere out there is a ranch that's sprung up out of nowhere and grown faster than some of the spreads that have been in Texas for years. We find that ranch, we'll find a lot of those stolen cattle."

Ramsey saw John Law was thinking hard about something. "You look like you got something on your mind there, Mister Law. Care to share it with us?"

"The night Charlie Beal was killed he told me a story about a poker game. The name Captain Jack and San Antonio came up during that game. Think about it. You steal a thousand head of cattle from Waco, drive the herd to a ranch somewhere in between that ranch and the border. Hold them there for a few weeks to let things die down, cut out a few hundred for yourself, then run the rest across the border and sell them in Mexico. That ranch grows in size and serves as a way station for stolen cattle at the same time. A damn smart setup if you think about it. The bought lawmen steer everyone away from the rustlers, giving them time to make it to the ranch. They hole up there while the Rangers roam all along the border watching for a big herd headed for the Rio Grande. But they don't have the men to keep that up for long. Two or three weeks later, after they've cleared out, you run 'em across."

Harrison shook his head. "You're right about one thing, J.T. This Captain Jack is a smart fellow, all right. Sounds like he's got this thing organized down to the brass tacks. I think you boys need to talk to Jenkins and this breed, Choctaw Jones."

Ramsey agreed. "Why don't you come to my office tomorrow, J.T. We can see what this Choctaw Jones has got to say when he finds out you killed all his friends."

"I'll be there."

"Well, getting late. I better be headin' back. Glad to hear Josh is gonna pull through, General. I'll be seein' you all."

As Ramsey started out the barn door, Harrison called to him.

"Hey, Heck, I got some folks from the capitol comin' for a little party tomorrow night. You're invited. Governor might even show up. What'd you say?"

Ramsey smiled, "Hell, General, you know I ain't no good around you political boys. But I got to admit, havin' that many crooks in one room is mighty damn tempting. See you."

The fact that the crusty old lawman had called him J.T. rather than Mr. Law hadn't gone unnoticed by the bounty man.

"Well, son," said Harrison, "you sure have a way of drawin' plenty of action whenever you're around. I wanta thank you for what you done for Josh. The young man's like the son I never had. Would have killed me to wire his pa that he was dead. I take it you and Jed got things worked out?"

J.T. seemed surprised as he replied, "You knew about that?"

"Ain't nothin' goes on around my ranch that I don't know about, son. Jed's a good man. Glad you all settled up."

As the pair left the barn, J.T. replied, "Yes he is, General—and a damn good shot with a Spencer rifle."

"RICH! RICH, ARE you in there?"

There was no answer. Taking a match from his vest pocket, Ramsey dragged it across the wood until it flared to life. Reaching his hand slowly through the doorway, he peered inside. The small flame didn't provide much light, but enough for the marshal to make out the figure of a man laying facedown on the floor. He couldn't tell who it was, but he had a good idea.

Ramsey knew the office like the back of his hand. When the match went out, he moved quickly into the room. He stayed close to the wall, away from the windows. Crouching low, he inched his way along the wall to the rifle rack. Next to it was a small table with a lamp. Reaching up in the darkness, he removed the glass globe and set it aside. With the pistol ready, he lit another match. If anyone was still in the room this was when they would open fire. Nothing happened. Lighting the wick, he placed the globe back on the lamp and turned up the light. Just as he had feared, the body on the floor was Rich. A pool of blood spread out from around his head. It was clear the young deputy was dead.

Keeping the gun at the ready, Ramsey picked up the lamp and carefully moved to the door leading to the jail cells. Choctaw Jones had been in the first cell. Now the cell stood open and empty. Placing the lamp on his desk, Ramsey knelt down next to Rich. The boy had been shot in the back of the head. Placing his hand on Rich's back, he rubbed gently as he fought back tears and whispered, "I'm sorry, son. I should've known better. You were always too trusting. But as God is my witness, I swear, I'll kill the man who did this to you."

Leaving the office, the marshal woke the undertaker, and

together they moved Rich's body to man's back room. Ramsey paid him fifty dollars and told him he wanted the best money could buy for the boy. Seeing how badly the marshal had been affected by the loss, the undertaker refused the money. Rich had died protecting the town. There would be no charge for the service. Ramsey thanked the man and returned to his office.

Sitting at his desk, Ramsey pulled a bottle from the drawer. Pulling the cork, he didn't bother with a glass. He tipped the bottle up and took a long pull on the whiskey. It burned all the way down, but he hardly noticed. His eyes were focused on the blood that stained his office floor. The blood of an excitable young man whose only ambition was to one day be as good a lawman as Heck Ramsey.

The longer he stared at the blood the more anger he could feel building within him, until finally he knew what he had to do. Going to the weapons rack he pulled down the short double-barrel shotgun. Shoving a handful of double odd buck into his pocket, he left the office and began walking down the middle of the street. He was headed straight for Sheriff Joe Wright's office at the end of the block. Ramsey was convinced that Wright had something to do with all of this. He may not have pulled the trigger, but he knew who did. And where was Choctaw Jones? The fat little bastard was going to tell him that too before he was through with him.

Nearing the sheriff's office, he saw the lamps burning through the windows. Good. For once the man was where he was supposed to be instead of in a bar or already laid up in bed. Stepping up onto the boardwalk, Ramsey kicked the door open and stepped inside, the shotgun leveled, the hammers back. There was no one there. The place was empty. "Dammit all to hell," he uttered. "Guess I'll have to hunt him down."

Walking out the door, the marshal paused for a moment to consider which saloon to go to first. Then he heard Joe Wright call out his name.

"Hey Ramsey! Lookin' for me?"

Ramsey turned to his left. Wright was standing at the corner of the alleyway next to his office. Half hidden in the shadows, he had a shotgun in his hands. At the same moment another voice called out. This one came from behind Ramsey.

"Hey, Marshal. Guess you'd be lookin' for me, too."

Ramsey knew it was the breed. He started to turn but Jones already had his gun out and the hammer back. The shot was loud. The bullet caught Ramsey in the left side, went down and came out at his right hip, knocking the lawman down. Ramsey tried to bring the shotgun around, but there was another roar and a second bullet shattered his right wrist. The shotgun dropped down across his legs. The pain was terrible. But he wouldn't give it up. Struggling to grip the scatter gun with his left hand, he tried to raise it and point it in the breed's direction. The breed began to laugh.

"Goddamn, Marshal, yer a tough ol' bird, I'll give ya that."

Jones fired again; this bullet shattered Ramsey's left wrist. The shotgun dropped and rolled onto the boardwalk. Looking toward the alley, Jones called out to Wright.

"That make it easy enough for ya, or are ya worried he might kick ya to death?"

Ramsey could hardly see, the pain was so bad. He turned his head toward the alley and saw Wright step up onto the boardwalk. He walked up to Ramsey and stood over the wounded man. There was smirk on his face as he said, "Ya was always lookin' down yer nose at me, ya sonofabitch. Well ya ain't so damn much now, are ya, Heck Ramsey."

Ramsey looked up at the little man and spat, "You go to hell, Joe Wright."

"Not tonight, Marshal."

Joe Wright pulled the trigger on the shotgun and blew Heck Ramsey's head apart.

THIRTEEN

✦

IMMEDIATELY FOLLOWING BREAKFAST the servants began to prepare the house for the upcoming party. J.T. went upstairs to visit with Josh, who was still in a lot of pain. The laudanum the doctors had left quickly took the edge off that, but made the young ramrod a little incoherent at times. He only stayed for a short time, then went back downstairs. Lucy followed him out onto the porch.

Looking into his eyes, she said, "John, I can't . . ."

Law raised his hand. "Lucy. Really. You don't have to keep thanking me all the time. You've already done that. Josh is hurt, but he's a strong man and he'll be cussing and drinkin' again in no time. You don't have to worry anymore."

Bowing her head like a scolded child, she spoke softly.

"I'm . . . I'm sorry. I don't mean to upset you. It's just that Josh means so much to me. If it hadn't been for you I would have lost him forever. You are such a strange man, John Thomas. I mean, you have this reputation as such a hard man. A gunfighter who has killed. The mere mention of your name puts fear into the hearts of other men. It's almost like you want people to fear you. To see you as some sort of deadly predator that has no heart or soul. Who never shows emotion or feeling. But I know better. I saw it in your face when you and Jed Davis rode in yesterday afternoon. You weren't concerned about yourself or how bad you might be hurt. Your only concern was Josh."

Stepping closer to him, she took his hand in hers. "I see what the others don't, John. Inside this chest beats the heart of a man who truly does care about others. A gentle man who longs for more in his life than guns and killing. Just as you are all those things to people when you wear a gun, think of all you could be without it. Have you even known real peace in your life, John? There is such a thing, you know. A home, a family. It's out there John, maybe even closer than you know."

John stared down into her blue eyes. They were like reflecting pools. Her words were beginning to have an effect on him. He could see her at the door of their ranch, hear the children playing in the yard. What more could a man want? Maybe she was right. All that stood between him and the peace she offered was a gun.

"Lucy, I . . ."

"Go on, John. Let the inner man, the caring, peace-loving man that I know is inside you speak."

Her firm young body was pressing against him. The scent of her perfumed hair so fresh, so intoxicating. The full red lips. Lips that at this moment were mere inches from his own. She closed her eyes and he kissed her. Gently at first, then stronger. She placed her hands on his broad shoulders and returned the kiss. It was a warm, passionate kiss that threatened to engulf them both. He had never know such a feeling, even when he was with Sara Jane. Their lips parted and she placed her head against his chest.

"This is the man I see, John Thomas. A gentle, warm man who is at peace with himself."

He was about to say something to her when Jed Davis came riding up to the house like the devil himself was on his trail. J.T. eased away from Lucy as Jed swung down out of the saddle so fast that he ran into the hitching rail.

"Heck Ramsey's dead! Him and that young deputy of his. Both of 'em."

J.T. couldn't believe it. The general came out onto the porch.

"What's all the commotion out here?" he asked.

Jed repeated himself. "Heck Ramsey's dead, General. That young deputy of his, too."

The news had a similar effect on Harrison. A look of disbelief crossed his face.

"How? When?" asked John Law.

"Best I could put it together it happened last night about ten, they figure. Folks heard shootin' but that late at night wasn't nobody brave enough to go see what it was right away. Ramsey found his man dead at the jail. The cells were empty. Ramsey took the boy over to the undertaker then went lookin' for that fellow he had locked up."

"He must have found him," said Harrison.

"Naw, he must have come up against two men, General."

J.T. stepped off the porch. "Why do you say that, Jed?'

" 'Cause whoever broke that fellow out of jail shot the deputy in the back of the head. When they found Ramsey he . . ."

Jed stopped for second and looked up at Lucy. "Ma'am, you might wanta go on inside. I don't think you'd wanta hear this."

She looked at J.T. then the general, who said, "Please, Lucy. If you don't mind."

She nodded and went inside. Jed continued with his story.

"When they found Ramsey, he'd been shot all to hell. Bullet in the side and one in each wrist. Then the bastards finished the job with a damn shotgun. Blew his head off."

Both of John Law's hands balled into a tight fist. He could feel the blood in his body beginning to boil as if there was fire alive in his gut.

"What'd Sheriff Joe Wright have to say about it?" asked Harrison.

Jed shook his head from side to side. "That's the queer part. Ain't nobody seen him. It's like he just up an' vanished. Hell, with Ramsey's two other deputies gone, there ain't no lawmen at all in Waco right now. Mighty strange. Yes, sir. Mighty strange."

Harrison turned to J.T. "You want me to get some of the men and come with you?"

"No, that's all right. You've got those folks comin' from Austin. If Jed's willing to go along, that's all the help I'll need."

Jed didn't hesitate. "Let me get another horse. I done blowed this one out. Won't take but a few minutes. How about your horse?"

"Already got him. Take your time, Jed. We'll get there soon enough."

Harrison shook his head. "This sure isn't going to look good if the governor does show up here tonight. A marshal killed in the street. A jail break, a deputy dead, a sheriff missing and a town the size of Waco with no lawmen. No, sir. Not good at all."

The anger was clear in J.T.'s face. "I don't really give a damn how it looks or what the goddamn governor thinks. Josh was right. Sometimes you have to take the law into your hands and deal with the bastards on their own terms. That's what I'm going to do. I owe Ramsey that much."

Harrison wasn't going to try and stop J.T. Normally a stronger backer of law and order with faith in the court justice system, he found it hard to find fault with John Law's anger. Heck Ramsey had been a longtime friend and a damn good man. He didn't deserve to die like that. Like Jed had said, right now there was no law in Waco. As he prepared to go back in the house, the general turned and looked at John Thomas. There was determination in the face, fire in the eyes and vengeance in his heart.

"You do what's got to be done, John T."

Jed rode up to the front steps. "You ready?"

J.T. stepped up into the saddle. Lucy came to the doorway. He saw a sadness in her eyes. That other man was back. Turning the buckskin, he told Jed, "Let's go."

● ● ●

JACK CORBIN WAS in his bedroom packing some things for his trip to Waco. As he did so he couldn't help but think how ironic life could be sometimes. He'd received a telegram from his friends in Congress. They wanted him to meet one of their party's most influential and trusted political advisers. Although no longer a member of the Senate, he was a powerful man with powerful friends. An endorsement from this man would practically guarantee Jack Corbin would be the next Attorney General of Texas. That man was the former general and retired senator The Honorable Tom Harrison.

Corbin would be leaving by train for Waco in two hours. He would be there by the afternoon and having drinks in the living room of the same man he had stolen cattle from less than two weeks ago. If that wasn't ironic he didn't know what was.

Carrying his satchel out onto to the porch, Corbin's mind was occupied with thoughts of the grand reception he would have in honor of his election. He hardly noticed Deke Toban walking up the hill toward the house. It was only when the big man shouted at him in his gruff, gravely voice that Corbin acknowledged his presence.

"What the hell is goin' on, Jack!"

Corbin stared blankly at the man, having no idea what he was yelling about.

"Don't give me that look ya lyin' pile of dog shit!" Holding a piece of paper in the air, Deke waved it in around and continued, "This here's a wire from Choctaw Jones. Frank Boyd, Quincy Cole and them other boys are all dead! What the hell have ya done, Jack?"

Corbin couldn't believe what he'd just heard. It wasn't possible. Toban had to be mistaken. How could this have happened?

"Yer not sayin' nothin', Jack! Why'd ya have Frank lie to me? An' what the hell are ya doin' sendin' people after a man like J.T. Law any damn way? Say somethin', damn ya!"

Reaching out, Corbin snatched the telegram from Deke's hand. Jones had had Wright code the message for him and Jenkins send it. Breed went on to tell how he'd been arrested. That Wright had broken him out. They had killed a marshal and a deputy, and both men were now in hiding outside Waco waiting for him to arrive, for further instructions.

Corbin was furious. "That idiot Joe Wright and your damn brother are to blame for this, Deke. Thought we could handle it in a quiet and reasonable manner. Now look at the mess we got on our hands."

At the mention of his brother's name, Deke was up the steps and in Corbin's face before the man stopped talking.

"What's my brother got to do with this, Corbin?"

"He's dead, dammit! That's what." Corbin hadn't meant to blurt it out like that, but the man had kept pushing him.

Deke's big hand shot out and grabbed the front of Corbin's shirt.

"Yer lyin' again, ya sonofabitch!"

"I wish I was, Deke. Buck and Kline were both killed by J.T. Law three nights ago. Frank was worried that you'd go crazy when you heard and do something foolish, so he took some boys to Waco to try and grab Law and bring him back here for you."

Deke slowly removed his hand. "So Buck really is dead?"

"Yes, Deke. I'm sorry. Guess we should have told you up front. You couldn't have caused any more of a mess than we got right now."

Corbin went on to tell Deke about the earlier message from Wright. That he was afraid J.T. Law was on to them, especially him. Things were starting to fall apart in a hurry. Corbin told him they had to find a way to keep it all together until after the election. As attorney general he would be the chief law official in Texas. Then they could do whatever they wanted.

Deke took a step back and nodded in agreement. Jack was right.

"I'll be goin' with you to Waco. Me and some of the boys. We'll take care of John Law and that damn Joe Wright. Ya just handle them politic fellows and stay clear of all this. Can't have your good name bein' linked to any of what's goin' on. That'd upset the whole damn plan for sure."

Corbin was impressed. Maybe he had misjudged Deke Toban. Perhaps the man had finally seen the advantage to having political power and position that he had been preaching to him from the very beginning.

"Okay, Deke. You pick your men. We'll leave within the hour."

The big man went down the steps and headed for the bunkhouse. His dead brother was on his mind. That, and ideas about all the ways he could kill John Thomas Law.

FOURTEEN

★

THERE WERE PEOPLE everywhere in the streets of Waco,
all talking about the terrible murders of two lawmen that had
occurred in their town. All anyone knew for sure was that
Heck Ramsey and his deputy were dead. A prisoner was
missing, and no one could find the sheriff. The judge of the
county had wired Austin, relaying the events and requesting
that the deputies with the prison wagon return to Waco immediately after their arrival. Until then, he had appointed a
temporary marshal.

The man's name was Cory Todd. He was about Josh's
age. He had been a friend of the marshal's and rode in a few
posses with Ramsey, so he had some experience. But nothing
had prepared him for the man that now stood in front of his
desk. The eyes were cold and hard. Todd knew who he was
and it scared the hell out of him. His request had been a
simple one. He wanted Todd to deputize him and Jed Davis.
It was something J.T. had thought about while they were
riding into Waco. The judge's quick action in appointing
Todd had been a smart move and showed the man's dedication to law and order. Not that it was going to stop John
Law from doing what he had intended all along, but since

there was law in Waco, wearing a badge would make the mayhem he had in mind legal, in a crude sort of way. It would sit better with the general as well.

Law and Davis waited while Todd tried to figure out what to do. His decision didn't really matter much. If he gave them the badges, fine. If not, then they would still do what they wanted and Todd could try to arrest them if he thought he could. At the moment that didn't seem to be an option he cared to think about.

Looking up from his desk into those hard eyes, Todd ask, "Do I have the authority to make you deputies? I mean, I'm just temporary."

"You're the marshal, right!" snapped J.T. "Appointed and sworn in by a judge. Hell, yes. You can just about do any damn thing you want. Now do we get the badges or do we handle things on our own and wait for you to come arrest us?"

The thought of having to try and arrest John Thomas Law was enough to make Todd pull open a drawer and remove deputy marshal badges. He had both men raise their right hand, then using a paper he had found in the desk, swore then both in as peace officers. When he had finished, Todd asked, "What do we do now?"

"*We* don't do anything. You stay here and do whatever paperwork lawmen do. Mister Davis and I will take care of everything else. You understand?" said Law.

"Yes, sir. Uh, I mean yes, Mister Law."

J.T. managed a slight smile. "Relax, son. You done made your first decision as a lawman, and it was a damn wise one at that."

Todd nodded his appreciation and watched the two men as they walked to the door. J.T. stopped and looked back at the young man.

"Marshal, if you should happen to see a group of rough-looking strangers ride into town, you come and find us. Don't you mess with them, you hear?"

"Yes, sir."

As the door closed behind the two men, Todd slumped back in his chair. One hour on the job and he was already

convinced that this was not his line of work. He didn't have
the nerves or the bladder control for it.

"Where we goin' first?' asked Jed.

"The telegraph office and Mr. Jenkins."

There were two men waiting and a woman at the counter
when the pair walked in. Jed whispered something to the
men and they quickly went out the door. Jenkins looked up
from the counter and saw J.T. staring at him. When he saw
the badge on the gunfighter's chest, his knees went weak and
he almost passed out.

J.T. addressed the lady at the counter.

"I'm sorry, ma'am, but the telegraph office is closed.
You'll have to come back later."

The woman turned to J.T. and frowned. "Well, I never.
You can't just walk in and run people out of a business
establishment like this. I waited in line ten minutes to get up
to this counter. I'm not leaving until this man accepts my
telegram. I don't care if you are a deputy marshal."

J.T. saw a grin appear on Jed's face. As if to say, "Brother,
she put you in your place."

J.T. saw panic in Jenkins's eyes. In an effort to appease
the gunfighter, Jenkins quickly said, "Ma'am. You'll have to
come back later."

The woman began to wag her finger at Jenkins. "Now you
look here. I won't—"

"Take the lady's telegram, Jenkins. You might not be able
to later," said J.T.

His hand visibly shaking. Jenkin's took the paper and
placed it next to the telegraph key. When he turned back
around the woman was still there.

"Well, how much do I owe you?" she asked.

"No charge, ma'am," said Law. "Since we inconvenienced
you, the city will pay for it."

"Oh my. Why, thank you. Good day, gentlemen."

Jed closed the door and flipped the CLOSED sign in the
window. Jenkins began to back away from the counter. J.T.
leaned forward and grabbed the trembling man by the front
of his shirt and jerked him forward into the edge of the
counter.

"Where's Joe Wright?"

Jenkins was so scared he could hardly talk. "I . . . I don't know. Why you askin' me?"

J.T. slapped the man hard across the face with his open hand.

"I don't have the time or the patience to put up with your lyin' bullshit, Jenkins. I know you and Wright are workin' for Captain Jack. So stop wastin' my time. Now where the hell is Joe Wright?"

Jenkins's eyes were watering. The left side of his face had gone bright red from the blow.

"I swear to God, I don't know. Him and another man pulled me out of bed last night. They had me send a telegram to San Antonio. That's all I know. I swear."

"What'd it say?" asked J.T., tightening his grip on the man's shirt.

Jenkin's eyes grew wide. "Oh, God. I don't know what it said."

Law gave him another slap in the face. Harder this time.

"You sent a telegram and you don't know what it said? Is that what you're telling me?" J.T. slapped him again. "You better start remembering damn fast."

"It was sent in code, damn it. The man wrote it out and Wright coded it. I just sent it. I don't know what it said."

"Where's the code book?"

"Joe Wright took it with him when he left. Honest to God. That's all I know."

"How did the operator in San Antonio know who the message was for if it was in code?"

"He works for Captain Jack. When he receives the messages with certain names on them, he passes them on to someone else who decodes it and delivers it, I guess. I don't know. I only worked with Wright. I don't know anyone else involved. I swear I don't. Don't hit me anymore—please."

J.T. relaxed his grip on the man's shirt, but still held onto him. "One more question: What about the message I sent to Austin? Did you send it or not?"

"No. We coded it and sent it to San Antonio."

J.T. looked over at Jed who said, "This Captain Jack read

it, got nervous and sent six men up here after you."

For the first time, Jenkins offered some information on his own.

"That was part of it," said the man, his hands trembling. "But, you killin' Buck Toban was the main reason they come for you. Got that much from Wright the other night."

"The deputy that tried to tree Doc in The Bull's Head?" asked J.T.

"That's right. He's got a brother named Deke. Real hard case. Figure he's kinda like Captain Jack's right-hand man. They didn't know it was you who killed Buck. They was supposed to take the fellow who killed him back with 'em, but when they found out it was you, they figured it'd be hell of a lot easier to bushwhack you, then hogtie you. 'Pears they was wrong on both counts."

J.T. released Jenkins, then walked behind the counter. Pushing him down in a chair, J.T. had the man send a message to Covington in Austin. In it, he told the Ranger what was going on in San Antonio at the telegraph office and how it was all linked to the outlaws. It was the break they were looking for. He would work on finding Joe Wright, while the Rangers worked on the San Antonio operator. Between them, J.T. was sure they could start unraveling clues to Captain Jack and his operation. He would keep Covington informed of his progress.

The message sent, J.T. handed Jenkins over to Davis and told him to take the man to the marshal's office and lock him up, then have Todd get the other telegraph operator out of bed. Mr. Jenkins was no longer employed by the company. He was going to start checking the bars. If Joe Wright was still in town, they'd find him.

It was late afternoon by the time Law and Davis finished their sweep of the town. Joe Wright was nowhere to be found and no one had any idea where the man might be. Sitting their horses at the end of main street, near the railroad depot, Jed looked out across the vast expanse of Texas prairie.

"Looks like the little bastard's skipped out. Any idea where he might be runnin' to?" he asked.

Lighting up a cigar, J.T. tossed the match aside and leaned forward on his saddle horn.

"If he did take off for good, he could be headin' for San Antonio. Looks like that could be the location Captain Jack's workin' out of. But he's still got Choctaw Jones with him. Somethin' tells me they're still around here somewhere."

"How ya figure?" asked Jed.

J.T. blew a column of smoke from his lips before he answered.

"Two reasons. This Jack fellow is the type that when he gives an order he expects it to be carried out. No excuses. They were supposed to get rid of me. They failed. That's another word the captain don't wanta hear when he gives an order. As far as he's concerned, the order still stands. But he'll send more men next time. Second, if you just killed two local lawmen, would you stay around long enough to send a telegram before you hightailed it out town? I don't think so. But you might, if you knew you were going to get more help and all you had to do was hide out until that help arrived. I think that's exactly what Choctaw Jones did."

Jed shifted in his saddle and thought about what the bounty man had just said. It made sense. All they'd really accomplished was shooting Josh, killing Ramsey and a deputy, and lost five of their own men in the process. J.T. Law was still a thorn in their side and he was still alive and kicking. He looked over at the gunfighter.

"I imagine that Deke fellow will be leadin' the next bunch comin' after ya."

J.T. smiled at the older cowboy. "I figure you're right, and that don't bother me in the least, as long as he brings that damn Captain Jack along with him. Let's head on back to the ranch. Nothin' more we can do here."

Jed rubbed his badge to a high shine. "We're still deputies, right?"

"That's right. At least till this thing's settled. It'll ease the general's mind, too."

The two men heard a whistle. Looking down the track they saw the rising black smoke of the evening train in the distance.

"Reckon some of the general's political friends'll be on that train," said Jed.

Remembering Ramsey's last words, J.T. sadly replied, "Yeah. Be a lot of crooks in one room tonight."

"What's that?" asked Jed.

"Nothin', Jed. Let's ride."

FROM HIS SEAT next to the window, Jack Corbin casually watched two cowboys riding off in the distance. He never gave it a second thought; his mind was on the problem at hand. They had arrived at the train station early. Corbin paid for an extra boxcar to be added to the train to carry the horses belonging to Deke and his men. When the man had said a few men, Corbin had figured he meant five or six—Deke's idea of a few men was fifteen. Corbin had started to protest, but knew it would do no good. Besides, Deke said it himself: Corbin was having nothing to do with what was going to happen. If things went bad for Deke and his men, Corbin didn't know them. That was why Deke and his men weren't even in the same car. They were riding three cars back. Corbin had no association with any of them. That suited him just fine.

At the station, Corbin stepped from the train and headed straight for the Astor Hotel, one of the most exclusive in Waco. Deke and his men unloaded their horses. Keeping three men with him, Deke sent the remainder across the bridge, telling them to find a place to hold up two miles from town. He would scout around Waco to find out what going on, then join them in a few hours. Jones had said that they would contact Corbin once he got to Waco. Once that contact was made, Corbin would pass the information on to Deke, who would be waiting at The Bull's Head saloon, before he left for the Circle H. Corbin had made it clear that once Deke met up with Jones and Wright and this business was finished, he wanted the lawman killed. Deke had no problem with that.

Corbin took a bath and put on a new suit of clothes, then went down to the lobby. Four members of the nominating committee, all of whom had shared in his $75,000 contri-

bution, were just coming out of the hotel bar. They greeted
the rich Texas cattleman as if he were a longtime friend. The
$75,000 had just been enough to whet their appetite. There
would be more coming their way once they had him in office
and they knew that. The politicians had rented a double-size
carriage for the ride out to the Circle H. He was more than
welcome to join them. Corbin was tempted to take them up
on their offer—there were some details he wanted to work
out with them, but he couldn't. He had to wait for Jones or
Wright to make contact. Thanking them for their offer, he
begged off, saying he had to see an old friend first but that
he would see them at the Harrison party later.

Once they were gone, Corbin left the hotel and began
walking down Main Street. Jones hadn't said where or when
they would contact him, only that they would. Corbin figured
he had an hour before he would have to leave for the Circle
H. He hoped Jones would show up soon; he couldn't afford
to be late meeting the famed general.

Having strolled the length of one side of the street, Corbin
started back the other way. As he was passing the newspaper
office, a low voice coming from the alley called out his
name. He stopped. Looking around to see if anyone might
be watching, Corbin quickly stepped back into the darkness
and moved down the alleyway. Choctaw Jones stepped out
from behind some boxes.

"Hey, Cap'n. Good to see you."

"Wish I could say the same. Where's Wright?"

The breed spit. "The coward bastard's hidin' outside of
town, scared to death."

"Of what?" asked Corbin.

Breed laughed. "Hell, of you, the whole damn town and
that J.T. Law. Him an' another fellow were all over town
today lookin' for the little shit. I mean he's really scared,
boss. Especially since the new marshal made that bounty
man a deputy."

"What? They made a damn gunfighter who's killed more
than twenty men a deputy marshal?"

"Sure enough, an he's usin' that badge to shake a few trees
around here. Got that Jenkins fellow from the telegraph of-

fice locked up already. An' he let everybody in town know if they had anything to do with Wright, they'd be joinin' Jenkins, or worse."

Corbin shook his head. Jesus, what a mess, he thought. He didn't need all this aggravation right now. He was so damn close to getting his foot in the door of Texas politics. It was the first step on the road to the governor's chair. He suddenly found himself wishing they were all dead: J.T. Law, Joe Wright, Deke and his men, even Jones. But wishing wasn't going to solve anything.

"Where's J.T. Law now?"

"You'll be seein' him soon enough, Cap'n. He's out at the Harrison place. He'll be at that get-together tonight. Anybody come with you?" asked Breed.

"Deke and fifteen of the boys. He wants this John Law bad."

Choctaw's eyes narrowed and his face took on an evil look that even frightened Corbin. "He ain't the only one. That bastard killed Frank and my friend Quincy. I wanta tie him to a tree an' cut on him slow and long. Make him scream for two days before I gut him."

There was little doubt in Corbin's mind that the half-breed Apache could do exactly that. "You go on across the bridge. Some of the boys are waiting for Deke two miles out of town. I'll send Deke and the others along soon as we figure out what we're going to do."

Choctaw faded away into the darkness of the alley. Corbin stepped back out into the street and headed straight for The Bull's Head. Meeting with Deke at a corner table, the two men discussed how they were going to handle J.T. Law.

"Well, you can't kill him at the house. We got to draw him out. How you want to deal with that?" asked Corbin.

Deke thought on it for a while but couldn't come up with anything at the moment. Corbin looked at his watch. He didn't have time to wait. He had to get going if he was going to be at the Circle H on time. "You think on it, Deke. Then do what you think is best. Just remember—whatever it is, it has to be done away from the house. I don't want Harrison or any of the guests there tonight caught in the middle of a damn shoot-out. That clear?"

Toban nodded that he understood and told Corbin to go ahead. He'd figure out something in the next couple of hours. Corbin left. Deke and his men waited twenty minutes, then did the same. Hooking up with Jones and the rest of the men, they followed the breed to an old abandoned mine where they found a badly frightened Joe Wright.

Seeing the men ride up and recognizing Jones in the lead, Wright came out of hiding to meet them. Deke reined in just short of the little man and stepped down from his horse. The sheriff walked toward him with his hand extended. But Deke wasn't interested in shaking hands. Taking two steps forward, he doubled up his fist and hit Wright with a vicious blow square in the face, sending the fat man to the ground like a poleaxed ox. He was out cold.

"That's for not watchin' after my little brother, ya sonofabitch!"

Stepping over Wright, Deke and the others went inside the mine. Jones broke out some whiskey and passed the bottles around. Deke stood up, and moving to the center of the circle, told the men why they were there, then asked if anyone had any ideas about how they could draw the man they wanted away from the ranch? One suggested they send a man in to tell J.T. the marshal had found something and wanted him to come into town. Another thought they should simply move in close to the ranch and watch. He was bound to ride out sooner or later, then they could ride him down.

Ironically, it was a dazed and bleeding Joe Wright who came up with the answer Deke liked the most. Staggering, the little man fell back against a wall and mumbled, "Ya ride down like yer ruslin' a herd. Let some of the punchers ride to the ranch for help. Law's sure to be the man leadin' the pack when they come to help out. Then ya ambush the whole bunch. When it's done an ya killed 'em all, ya still got the cattle as a damn bonus."

There was silence among the group as they looked at one another. As much as they hated to admit it, they liked the lawman's idea. Especially the part about keeping the cattle as a bonus. If they were going to match guns against a man like John Thomas law, they deserved something extra.

Deke walked across to Wright, who quickly put his hands up to fend off another blow from that massive fist. Deke laughed and wrapping his arm around the little man, said, "Damn good idea, lawman. Matter of fact, I'm gonna let ya lead this outfit on that raid tonight. What'd think of that?"

Wright quickly shook his head from side to side. "Oh, no. I couldn't do that."

"Hell ya can't. It's yer damn idea. Yer gonna ride all right—an' right out front. Time ya started earnin' all that money Jack's been payin' ya. Let's go, boys. Sheriff here's gonna show us how to rustle cattle tonight."

Laughing, the outlaws left the mine and headed for their horses. Deke practically threw Wright up on a horse next to him. Slapping his holster, he looked the scared little man in the eyes. "Ya try to run on me, lawdog, an' I swear to God I'll blow ya right outta that saddle. Ya hear what I'm sayin'?"

Wright nodded that he did. As they moved out, Wright was wishing he'd just taken his money and run like he'd started to do. Now it was too late and he had a bad feeling that J.T. Law and his men weren't the only ones who were going to die tonight.

FIFTEEN

✦

MUSIC CARRIED ON the night air as vaqueros sang to the strumming of Mexican guitars and the men and women of Waco, along with distinguished guests from the capitol milled about the porch, drinks in their hands, enjoying the music and pleasant conversation. Just as J.T. had figured, Harrison had been overjoyed at seeing the badges on Law and Davis when they returned to the ranch. Even Lucy had seemed surprised. After filling Harrison in on what had happened in town, the general told the men to get themselves ready for the night's events.

Jed wasn't much for fancy shindigs and told the general that if he didn't mind, he's just as soon forego the party in favor of some much-needed sleep. Harrison said that would be fine. But J.T. was not as fortunate. Word that the famed bounty man and gunfighter was at the residence had sparked the interest of many of the guests, who if not brave enough to engage him in conversation, would at least have the opportunity to see the man who had stood with Doc Holliday and engaged in a shoot-out on the streets of their very own city.

Then of course there was Lucy. She wasn't about to let

him miss a chance to socialize with Waco's elite. Perhaps it was her Northern upbringing that somehow made her believe that by doing so, John Thomas Law would see that there were more opportunities in life than simply being good with a gun. She was convinced that he could do what these men had done. He was smart. Through hard work and determination he could become a refined gentleman of means and a member of this same social club. All he needed was a strong woman to stand at his side. She was becoming more and more convinced that she was that woman.

One hour into the party, J.T. was wishing he'd kept his room at The Ambrose. He felt totally naked standing in a room without a single gun anywhere on him. But of course it was a social event; that and the fact that Lucy had insisted that he leave them upstairs. He watched her move about the room. Where he felt so out of place, she seemed to fit in perfectly among this crowd. More than a few of the men were impressed by her beauty and charm. She found it easy to talk with them and at same time smooth the feathers of their jealous wives with comments about their hair or lovely gowns. She really knew how to work a room. No doubt about that.

Harrison waved J.T. over to a corner where he was standing with five well-dressed men. The general had introduced him to practically everyone in the place; he had already forgotten most of their names. Hopefully, this would be the last. Forcing a smile, he joined them in the corner.

"Gentlemen. I'd like you to meet John Thomas Law. Presently serving as a deputy marshal for our little town."

Harrison went on to introduce the men, four of whom were congressional members of the House. The fifth was a tall, handsome sort of fellow who the general introduced as a Texas rancher. "J.T., this here is Jack Corbin. If things go well with the upcoming convention, Mr. Corbin here will be our next attorney general."

As John T. shook hands with the man they stared into each other's eyes. It was the first time tonight the gunfighter detected a hint of hostility. The smile was there, but the eyes told another story. It wasn't just a mere look of dislike, but bordered on the edge of pure hate.

"Where are you from, Mr. Corbin?" asked J.T.

"San Antonio, Mister Law. Have a rather large ranch down that way."

Every trusted instinct that J.T. possessed went on alert. He couldn't explain why. There were a lot of ranches and a lot of people in San Antonio. The man's name was Jack—hell, there were a lot of Jacks in Texas. What'd that prove? Still, there was something about the man that didn't sit well with John Law.

"Did you happen to be engaged in the late War Between the States, Mr. Corbin?" asked John T.

Corbin was about to answer when Lucy came over and slipped her hand around John Law's arm. She nodded to the gentlemen and said, "You promised me a dance, John Thomas Law. I'm calling in that promise now."

Corbin smiled. "By all means, Mister Law. Don't let us keep you from such a delightful experience."

J.T. got the feeling the man was trying to avoid his question.

"About the war, Mr. Corbin?"

Corbin raised his hand as if waving off the importance of his role in that bloody conflict. "Yes, I was, but it was a minor role, I assure you. Nothing worth mentioning. Really. Never cared much for military life, actually. Now if I were you, sir, I'd dance with this charming creature before half the men in this room try and take her away from you."

J.T. was about to ask another question when Lucy began pulling him away. As they began to dance J.T. continued to watch Corbin. There was just something about the man that didn't feel right. But apparently he was the only person in the room who seemed to feel that way. He watched the general laugh as the man made a comment. Harrison appeared to like him. He was obviously well educated, extremely pleasant, wealthy and trustworthy enough to be considered for the position of attorney general. All John T. had going up against all that was that damn sixth sense of his. But it had never failed him yet.

"John . . . John. Are you listening to me at all?" asked Lucy as they waltzed around the floor.

"I'm sorry. What were you saying?'

"I said, I was talking with Mister Bowers, president of the National Bank. He may have a position opening soon. I told him you might be interested. He was actually excited by the prospect of your presence at his bank on a daily basis. Do you think you may be interested?"

Corbin and two of the congressmen were walking out onto the porch when Lucy asked her question. J.T. had only heard part of what she had said.

"Oh, uh, yes. That sounds very nice, Lucy. Please excuse me. I have to speak to the general for a moment. Maybe you could check on Josh."

"He's doing fine. That medicine the doctors gave him allows him to sleep for hours, you know that. If I didn't know better J.T. Law, I'd think you were trying to avoid me."

J.T. didn't answer as he pulled away from her, leaving her standing alone in the crowd of dancers. "Oh, that man. Manners will have to be the first thing we work on."

J.T. walked up to Harrison. The general was in the middle of a conversation at the moment. J.T. waited patiently for him to finish. He had a few questions about Corbin's war record. There were few politicians that ran for office who didn't often embellish their service as a way to garner votes. Corbin had done just the opposite, relegating himself to no more than a mere paper-pusher. Hardly the type the general would support, but then he could be wrong. The war had been over a long time. Finally the man with Harrison left.

J.T. was about to ask the question when Jed came bursting into the room and yelled the general's name.

"Tom—Tom! Rustlers! They just hit the herd down by the river."

J.T. rushed past Harrison, saying, "I'll take care of it, General. You all go ahead with your party. Jed, have them saddle my horse."

"Doin' it now, John T."

Law rushed up the stairs to his room. When he came back

down he was strapping on his gun. Lucy yelled out to him as he hurried by her. "Be careful, John."

The two men rushed out of the house. Ten riders were waiting. One held John T.'s horse. Law leaped into the saddle. Just as he was about to swing out he saw Corbin standing on the porch. There was a sly grin on his face, as if he knew something the bounty man didn't. He still had a lot of questions for the man but there wasn't time right now.

"Let's go, boys!" shouted J.T. as he led the men of the Circle H toward the main gate. Harrison stood on the porch with a crowd behind him as they watched the men race across the prairie in the moonlight until they were out of sight. Turning to Corbin, Harrison said, "Once you're elected, Jack, I expect you to put a stop to this sort of thing."

Corbin nodded. "You can rest assured that I will, General."

As the crowd went back into the house, two of the congressmen lingered behind with Corbin. "We can rest assured, huh, Jack?" said one of them with a wink.

Jack replied, "That's right, Congressman. But of course we will have to allow for expenses, won't we? Putting a stop to crime of this sort can be very, very expensive. And who's to say where all that money goes, right?"

The three men were laughing as they walked back inside. Corbin paused a moment and looked out across the prairie. By morning his problems would all be over. No more J.T. Law. No more Joe Wright, and if he was really lucky and Law was as good as everyone said he was, no more Deke Toban.

Seeing Lucy near the door, Corbin went up to her and smiled.

"I wouldn't worry, Miss Kincade. Mr. Law appears to be very adept at handling situations such as this. I'm sure he will be fine."

She returned the smile as she said, "Do you really think so?" Placing a hand on her arm, Corbin replied, "Oh, of course. Now come. Let me get you some punch and maybe we can dance a time or two to take your mind off things for awhile."

• • •

"HOW MANY WERE there?" yelled J.T. as they rode toward the river.

"Hard to tell," said one of the drovers who had brought the warning. "There was a lot of shootin'. I saw maybe eight or ten guns. Could be more."

As they cut across the south range, heading for the valley and the river, Jed saw riders approaching from the right. "J.T.!" he yelled, and pointed in that direction.

Leery of an ambush, John T. brought his men to a halt as he stared into the darkness at the moonlit figures approaching.

"Be ready, boys. No tellin' who this might be."

"Jed! Jed Davis! That you?" came a voice from the dark.

Jed breathed easy. Looking to J.T. he said, "It's okay. That's Big Mike Brown and some of the ranchers. Musta been on their way to the big doin's tonight."

Brown and his group rode up to J.T. and waved. J.T. counted eleven riders.

"Where you boys goin' in such a hurry. The general's party all that bad?"

"Rustlers!" said J.T. "Hit the Circle H herd down by the river. Glad to see you boys. We can use the extra guns."

"Hell, what are we waitin' for? Let's get after the bastards!" shouted Big Mike.

J.T. liked the man's spirit. But then he figured that if he had lost a son to these outlaws, nothing would hold him back either. They were twenty-three now. He was betting the rustlers hadn't planned on that many. For once the odds were going to be in favor of the law and the ranchers.

Less than a mile from where the rustlers had struck, J.T. reined the men in. He then proceeded to split the group up. Keeping seven with him, he sent Jed and seven men around to the left, while sending Brown and six others down the river a mile where they would cross over then come back up until they were almost directly across from the main force. If J.T. had figured right, they could expect to be ambushed as soon as they closed the pursuit. Brown and his men were not to fire a shot, but rather wait for the fleeing rustlers to enter the water. Once they did, J.T. and the others would close in on them from behind. They would have the outlaws in a deadly crossfire from which none could escape.

As Jed and Brown rode off according to the plan, J.T. looked at the men left sitting on their horses around him.

"Okay, boys. We're gonna be the bait for this little dance. All I can tell you is be ready. Once the shootin' starts things are gonna be happenin' damn fast. If you're hit, find yourself some cover and hole up. We'll be back for you as soon as it's over. Ride hard and shoot straight, boys. Let's give 'em hell!"

Racing headlong into the valley that led to the river, John Law knew this was the perfect place for an ambush. With each stride the big buckskin made he expected to hear the sound of rifle fire. The moon wasn't quite at full, but bright enough for the men to make out the rocks, trees and rolling hills of the valley. As the sounds of their horses' thundering hooves carried along the slopes on the night air, the men rode tense in their saddles knowing full well that at any moment it would begin, and each praying that he would not be the first man knocked from his horse by hot lead.

The opening round of the battle came not as a single shot, but rather as a volley from the right slope. J.T. saw one of his men tumble from the saddle. He hit the ground, bounced and rolled in the dirt. Another let out a yell, and grabbing his arm, swung his horse toward the trees to escape the swarm of lead that flew around them like a nest of angry bees. A horse reared up then screamed as a bullet tore through its shoulder, tossing its rider to the ground, then ran away, trailing loose reins in the dirt. The cowboy leaped to his feet and scrambled for the rocks. Seconds later flashes from his six-gun were seen as he fired at the bushwhackers along the west slope.

Gunfire lit up the night as the volume of fire increased from every direction. J.T. and his men struggled to stay in the saddle, knowing that any second now Jed Davis and his men would be riding down on the outlaws to the west, from behind. They just had to hold on.

A bullet burned across J.T.'s leg, ripping his pants and cutting a half inch groove through his flesh. But he hardly noticed. The adrenaline was rushing though his body as it had during those terrible battles in Kansas and Missouri during the war. The flashing of guns, the roar of gunfire, screaming horses along with the cries and moans of men wounded and dying were all sounds from his past. He had been to Dante's *Inferno* before. Hell hadn't changed.

J.T. knew they couldn't stay mounted much longer. Another man went down. He was about to yell for his men to take cover when the volume of gunfire suddenly increased. Looking up the west slope he saw a line of riders crest the hill. A familiar Rebel yell came from Jed Davis as he and his men rode down the surprised bushwhackers.

On the east slope, Deke Toban was cussing as he reloaded his rifle. One of his men cried out, "Deke! Look—they got behind Choctaw an' his boys."

"Dammit!" shouted Toban, as he nervously looked back up the slope behind him expecting to see another horde of riders descending on his own men.

Joe Wright was in a panic. "We gotta git outta here! Hell, we didn't ambush them fellows—they trapped us! We gotta git, Toban, and now!"

"Shut up, ya goddamn coward! I gotta think," said Deke.

Across the way the outlaw leader watched as Law and his men swung their horses up the west slope, catching Jones and the others in wicked crossfire that was quickly taking its toll.

From out of the dark, one of the other men yelled, "What the hell is there to think about? We gotta ride 'fore we get cut off and surrounded our damn selves."

Toban knew the man was right. "Okay. Mount up! We'll make for the river."

"What about Jones?"

"Them boys are on their own. Ain't nothin' we can do for 'em now. Let's git the hell outta here."

Choctaw felt a sudden jerk on his shirtsleeve as a bullet tore though the cloth an inch from his elbow. Two of his men were dead and three others wounded and down. In the glow of the moonlight he saw Toban and his men making a break for it. The sonofabitch had wrote him and his men off and pulled out of the fight. They were caught in a crossfire of hot lead with mounted riders coming at them from the front and rear. It was only a matter of time before Law and his men rode right over them.

Encouraging his men to fight it out to the last, Jones fired a couple of shots in Law's direction, then ducked in among the rocks. While his men fought to stay alive, Breed began to crawl through the rocks until he came to the edge of some woods. Making a run for it, Choctaw made it into the trees only seconds before Davis and his men rode past him. Scrambling down the slope, Breed found a horse wandering about. Wisely, he didn't mount the animal, but instead, slowly walked alongside the horse, leading him away from the battle. Fifty yards away, he swung up in the saddle. The firing had stopped. J.T. Law had outsmarted them. Breed turned his horse north. He figured that Toban would break for the river. It was the quickest way out of the valley. He could catch up to them there.

J.T. moved among the bodies scattered along the west slope, searching for Joe Wright, but he wasn't there. Calling over to Jed, Law asked if they'd found anyone alive. The reply was no. Had they found the half-breed? Again the answer was no. The outlaws who had been deserted and left to fend on their own had fought to the last man. Outlaws or not, a man had to respect that kind of courage.

Mounting up, he yelled to the others. "Let's go, boys. They're headed straight for the river and Big Mike. We'll close the back door on 'em now."

As they approached the river, Toban felt nervous. This John Law was a smart fellow, and a brave sonofabitch to boot. He'd led his men into that valley knowing full well that they were going to be ambushed. That took plenty of nerve. Weren't many men around with that much sand anymore. What bothered Deke at the moment was the fact that he and his men had managed to ride out of that trap so easy. It was as if Law had purposely left the gate open for them to get away. Why would he do something like that?

Stopping fifty yards short of the river, Toban called two of his men forward.

"I want you two men to take our sheriff here and cross over and scout out the other side."

Wright rose up in his saddle to voice his objection to the idea, but before he could open his mouth, Toban pulled his .45 and leveled it at Wright's gut.

"Ya got somethin' ya wanta say?"

Wright meekly lowered himself back in the saddle and shook his head from side to side.

"Well, get goin' then. We'll be right behind ya."

The three men drew their guns and walked their horses into the water. Brush lined the bank. A thick grove of dark and forbidding trees covered the area beyond. Toban waited, expecting to see muzzle flashes any minute. But as the men exited on the other side, he began to wonder if maybe J.T. Law had spooked him so bad that he was losing his nerve. Still it wouldn't hurt to give them a few minutes to scout it out. But that idea quickly fell to the wayside as one of the men called out that he could hear horses coming up behind them.

"Let's get across, boys. We can make a stand on the other side if we have to," shouted Toban.

Men and horses rushed into the water. Halfway across, Deke searched ahead for Wright and the other two men. They were gone. This sent up an immediate warning to the veteran outlaw, but before he could yell out a warning, a flurry of gunfire erupted from the tree line. Three horses drifted downstream, their saddles empty.

The outlaws fired back, some of their shots finding their mark as they heard the screams of wounded men come out of the darkness. Muzzle flashes lit up the night. Roaring gunfire and splashing horses mixed with the desperate cries of men battling for their lives carried downstream on the night air.

Joe Wright suddenly broke from the trees, his horse leaping into the water, almost tossing the fat man from his saddle.

His eyes were wide with fear. Blood stained the left sleeve of his shirt and he screamed, "Help me! God almighty—somebody help me. I'm hurt."

The lawman found himself face to face with Deke Toban.

"Help me, Toban. They . . . they shot me. I'm the sheriff, for godsakes—an' they shot me."

The outlaw leader laughed at the lawman. "Ain't like shot-gunnin' a helpless fellow, is it, ya sonofabitch. Does it hurt?"

Wright had tears streaming down his face as he cried out, "Oh, God. Yes! Hurts bad."

"Well, let me help ya, then," said Toban, reaching out with his left hand. Wright did the same with his good arm. Amid all the confusion, the fat man felt he still might have a chance. But that illusion quickly faded as he looked down and saw the gun in Toban's right hand. It was pressed against his stomach.

"See ya in hell, ya sonofabitch!" Toban pushed the gun further into the man's gut and pulled the trigger three times. Wright cried out once, then dropped out of his saddle and into the water. A huge pool of blood instantly formed around the bobbing figure as it drifted into the bank.

Deke Toban suddenly felt a bullet rip along his side. Felt the warm flow of blood leak from his body. In desperation, he slipped out of the saddle and let the current carry him downstream. As he looked back, he saw what few men he had left turn their horses and make a break back to the south bank, only to meet with gunfire from Law and his men, who had suddenly reappeared.

Rolling over in the water, Toban struggled to make it to the bank, but the current was swift and the wound in his side had left him weak. He was about to resign himself to drown-ing when he felt a hand grab him by the back of his vest and pull him toward the bank. Once on shore, he rolled over and looked up into the face of Choctaw Jones. The breed still had money coming. Saving Deke Toban's ass would guarantee that he got that money.

"You stay put. I'll get you a horse," whispered Jones.

While he lay there, Toban could hear the men talking up-stream. There was excitement in their voices as they congratulated each other. They had finally dealt the outlaws a deadly blow. Someone called out John Law's name and said they had found Joe Wright. *Yeah*, thought Toban—*they found him all right, but the little coward won't be doing any talking now.*

Jones suddenly reappeared. Helping Toban to his feet, he managed to get the big man into the saddle and quietly lead him away from the river and back in the direction of the abandoned mine. As far as Jones knew, they were the only two men still left alive.

J.T. called out, asking his men if any of the outlaws were still breathing. But like their comrades on the slope, these men too had fought to the death. Looking down at the body of Joe Wright, John Law cussed under his breath. If only he'd gotten his hands on the little man like Josh had wanted to, Heck Ramsey would probably still be alive now. But what was done was done, there was no going back. Wright was dead and along with him, the name of the man behind all this.

Jed walked up and placed his hand on Law's shoulder.

"We stung 'em good, John Law."

"Not all of them, Jed. The breed is missing, and Big Mike says he saw the big fellow who shot Joe Wright take a bullet and drift downstream. Some of the others heard the name Deke Toban bein' shouted during the fight. I'm bettin' it was Toban who Mike saw floatin' away. We got to find them, Jed. With Wright dead, they're our only link to the boss of this outfit. Send some of the boys downstream. I know it's dark, but have a look anyway. Bein' hurt, he might have made it to the bank. We've got to get our hands on somebody who can talk."

Jed shouted orders to the men, telling Mike to take his crew down the north bank, while he and J.T. would take the others along the south side. If anyone found anything they would fire two shots. They would search for an hour, then meet back at the site of the battle in the valley. The search proved fruitless; Choctaw Jones and Deke Toban were long gone.

SIXTEEN

✦

J.T. LAW AND his men returned to the Circle H and were immediately cheered by those at the party when told of the total destruction of the rustlers. Cheered by all, that is, except Jack Corbin, who managed to put up a good front, but held his burning hatred of John Law in check for the moment. The man was like a bad dream that wouldn't go away. Nothing was working out as he had planned. Tactfully, Corbin milled among the returning heroes, listening as they told of the battle. The only good news was that Joe Wright was dead. The bad news was that he overheard others talking about a search for a half-breed and another man named Toban, who had been wounded but apparently got away. If this were true, there was a good chance Jones would try to contact him again. He had to get back to Waco.

Looking around the room for Harrison, he spied the general circled by a group of congressmen and ranchers. Easing himself into the group, Corbin waited for his chance to express his congratulations on the handling of the outlaws. He thanked Harrison for the opportunity to meet with him and his offer of support in the upcoming election. He then expressed his regrets, but he wasn't feeling well and thought it best that he return to his hotel. Harrison offered the assistance of his doctor friends, but Corbin assured him that was not necessary; he was sure it was nothing but fatigue from the long train ride. He'd be better after some much-needed sleep.

"Well, then, perhaps we can have dinner tomorrow at the hotel. That is, if you are up to it of course," said Harrison.

"That would be fine, sir. Hopefully you can bring Miss Kincade with you. But given the situation with her brother, I could understand if she chose not to attend."

"I'll talk with her about that. She seems to enjoy your company," said the general.

"Fine. Thank you again, sir. I'll see you tomorrow."

With that Corbin excused himself and quickly left for Waco. He couldn't help but worry. Deke Toban had been a hard man to handle from the beginning—a wounded Deke Toban was like having a loose cannon on deck. No telling what he'd do now. It would have been better for him if Toban had been killed along with Joe Wright, but that wasn't the case. All Corbin could do now was try and contain the damage that had been done. One thing was certain: John Thomas Law wasn't going to simply go away because they had killed a bunch of rustlers. He was like a wolf that had picked up a scent, and he was determined to follow that scent until it eventually lead to Jack Corbin. The only thing that was going to stop that wolf was a bullet.

Back at the party, J.T. had been upstairs to see Josh. He told the foreman about the fight and the destruction of the outlaws. The news seem to lift the young man's spirits. Still in considerable pain, Lucy administered some more laudanum and he quickly drifted off into a sound sleep. As the couple came downstairs, Law was looking for Corbin. He still had some questions for the man, but he didn't see him anywhere. Seeing the general on the front porch he asked his host where Corbin was.

"Oh, he's already left, John. Said he was tired from his trip, but we're supposed to have dinner with him tomorrow night at his hotel. Why? Is there something wrong?"

"Oh, no, sir. That's all right. We had been talking about

the war earlier. He seemed to be a bit shy about his time in the service. I was just curious as to why that was, that's all. A lot of men in politics play their wartime service right up front when they're lookin' for votes. Not Mister Corbin. Just found that strange, I guess."

J.T. saw a frown appear on Harrison's face. "Now, John. That war's been over a long a time. Just because Jack Corbin's a Yankee who settled in Texas and made somethin' of himself is no reason to suspect him of anything. He had a brilliant record as an officer during the war. Hell, he was with Custer's command. Rode with Custer in plenty of battles, even got wounded in the fight at Brandy Station. He could toot his own horn if he wanted to, I reckon. But he's got enough sense to know better. But why alienate the voters? The war's over, true, but it's not forgotten by a long shot. Corbin knows that, so he don't talk about it much, that's all. Lot of men do that. Look at yourself. Since I met you, I'll bet you haven't said more then ten words about what you did during the war."

J.T. Law felt as though he had just struck gold. Corbin was an ex–Yankee officer, and a cavalry officer at that. He had served under a man known for his military tactics during the war. Add in the fact that his name was Jack and he had a large ranch outside of San Antonio. Then the same day he arrives in Waco, Deke Toban and his boys show up, breaking their usual pattern for rustling cattle. When it was all put together it was too much for John Law to consider as pure coincidence. In his own mind, John Thomas Law was convinced that Jack Corbin was Captain Jack.

But he was going to have to tread lightly until he could prove that theory. Corbin aspired to be the next Attorney General of Texas and had the backing of some of the most powerful people in the state—General Tom Harrison included. What he needed was proof—the talking kind. Someone who could point the man out in front of witnesses. So far all that J.T. had managed to come up with were dead men. It was proof positive of the old saying, "Dead men tell no tales."

• • •

THE FOLLOWING MORNING, J.T. and Davis took some
of the men from the H back out to the site of the battle.
While the drovers buried the dead, J.T. conducted another
search of the area. He found nothing on the west slope. At
the river he told the men to put Wright's body over a saddle;
he would take the former sheriff into Waco. While they buried the others, he and Jed Davis scouted downstream. They
were about to head back when J.T. noticed blood on the
brush along the bank. A closer look found more blood, boot
prints and the tracks of one horses near the bank, then farther
out, sign that a second horse had been brought up. Dried
blood could be seen where the horses had been mounted.

Jed looked at J.T. "Guess now we know why we didn't
find the breed or that fellow Toban."

J.T. studied the tracks, then off to the west. He told Davis
to finish up at the river, then take Wright's body into the
marshal's office. He was going to follow the tracks. Davis
started to argue that he should go along, but Law told him
he could handle this alone. As Jed mounted to leave he told
John Law to remember one thing: A wounded snake was
twice as deadly.

By late in the afternoon, Law had trailed the two sets of
tracks to a location five miles west of town. As Toby picked
his way among the rocks that led down into a dry riverbed,
J.T. heard the distinct whinny of a horse. The animal was
close. Pulling his rifle from his boot, J.T. slipped out of the
saddle and quietly moved up the dusty creek bed. Moving
up the north side, he peered over a slight ridge and saw two
horses standing near the entrance to an old mine. As best as
he could tell, that entrance was the only way in or out.

He wasn't sure who was inside. More than likely it was
Choctaw Jones and Deke Toban. But whoever it was, they
had been at the river last night and now he had them backed
into a corner. That might not be the best thing. A cornered
man was more likely to fight harder out of pure desperation,
and J.T. needed at least one of these men alive if he hoped
to prove his case against Corbin. For the moment they had

no idea he was there. These weren't the kind of men who were going to throw up their hands and surrender. He knew that. They had already proved that the night before. He decided he would wait for a while to see if they came out. One of them was wounded. J.T. didn't know how bad, but from the blood he'd found, it was bad enough that sooner or later the man was going to need a doctor. The only medical help around was in Waco. If they were going to try for a doctor, it would come later, when they could sneak into town under the cover of darkness. J.T. decided to take that gamble and wait them out.

AS THE SUN slowly began to set in the west, Tom Harrison helped Lucy up into a buggy for the ride into town. She had decided to accept Corbin's offer to join them for dinner. At the marshal's office, Jenkins's replacement came in with a telegram addressed to John Thomas Law. He gave it to Marshal Todd, then left. The young lawman wasn't sure what he should do with it. He was by himself and it was suppertime. There was a chance J.T. Law would be in town tonight. He'd give it to him them; if not, he'd take it out to the ranch tomorrow. Tossing it down on the desk, Cory Todd grabbed his hat and went to eat. As he was crossing the street he couldn't help but wonder why a gunman like John Thomas Law would be getting a telegram from Ranger Headquarters in Austin.

THE SUN HAD set and the darkness was beginning to close in around John T. There had not been a sound or any sign of movement from the mine. But now, as night began to fall he saw a faint glow of flickering light near the entrance. Someone had lit a candle. Sound carries farther at night, and Law could make out the sound of voices coming from the opening. It sounded as if they were arguing, but he was too far away to make out what the men inside were saying. Climbing over the brim, John Law was quietly making his way across the open ground when suddenly he saw shadows moving in the candlelight. He dropped to the ground within fifty feet of the mine.

He had already levered a round into the chamber of the rifle. As the two men appeared at the entrance, he brought the weapon up. He could have easily killed both men in a matter of seconds, but that wasn't his purpose. He needed one of them alive. A wounding shot would have worked in the daylight, but from this distance and the poor lighting, it would be near impossible. He couldn't take the chance. Lowering the rifle, he watched as one of the men helped the other into the saddle. After mounting his own horse, he took the wounded man's reins and began leading him toward town.

J.T. hurried back over the brim and down into the riverbed. Shoving the rifle back in his boot, he swung up on Toby and began to follow the outlaws, remaining back a safe distance to avoid detection. He wasn't worried about losing them; he knew exactly where they were going. He'd take them on in town where there was better light and he could make use of his expertise with a Colt. .45.

SETTING HIS HORSE at the edge of town, Choctaw Jones surveyed the street. There were too many people moving around for them to go in that way. Circling around to the east, he led Toban's horse past the livery stable and into an alleyway across from the doctor's office. They were in luck. There was still a lantern burning inside. Easing Deke out of the saddle, he placed an arm around his neck and slowly walked him across the street to the front door. Peering inside Jones saw the doctor closing his medical bag and preparing to blow out the light. Turning the doorknob and kicking the door open, he shouted to the startled medicine man.

"Hey—help me, Doc. My friend's been hurt bad. Accidentally shot himself."

The doctor set his bag down and rushed over to help Breed. Leading Deke to the couch, the doctor quickly opened his shirt and examined the wound.

"Peculiar place for a fellow to shoot himself," said the doctor as he jecked open his medical bag.

Breed had moved to the door and quickly closed it. He was now looking out at the street through the edge of the curtain. "Yeah, Doc. I know. He's kind of clumsy when it comes to guns. How bad is it?"

The doctor nodded. "Most men are, it seems. Oh, it's not really all that bad. More painful than anything else. Seems to have lost a lot of blood, but the bullet went clean through. Few stitches and a week in bed, he'll be fine."

"That's good, Doc. Could you hurry it up?"

Looking at the breed suspiciously, the doctor began to get the feeling that something wasn't right about all this. "What's your hurry?"

Jones thought for a second then looking back at the medical man he replied, "Got to get him back to Austin, to his sister's place. We got tickets for the late train."

That made sense to the doctor, who now felt a little silly. "Have him ready to travel in ten minutes. There's some whiskey on my desk there if you'd like a drink."

J.T. had left Toby at the end of the alley. Staring across at the doctor's office, he saw Jones leave the window and cross the room. Now was his chance to cross the street without being seem. Stepping lightly up onto the boardwalk, J.T. drew his Peacemaker and inched his way toward the window. Looking inside, he saw Toban stretched out on the couch. His gun belt lay on the floor a few feet away. The doctor was sewing him up. Jones was at the desk pouring himself a drink. Now was his chance. He might have to kill Jones, but he knew he could get to Toban before the man could reach his gun.

J.T. was about to kick open the door when a loud voice coming from behind him yelled out, "Hey, you! What are you doin' there?"

Law turned to see Ramsey's two dust-covered deputies, their guns pointing at him. Having received the message that Ramsey had been killed they had ridden straight through from Austin.

"Drop that gun, mister!" shouted one of the lawman.

There was a suddenly flurry of activity from the doctor's

office, then the lantern went out. "Dammit all to hell!" said
J.T.

"Drop it, mister! We ain't gonna say it again,"

"You don't understand. The men that helped kill Ramsey
are in there. They'll get away if you don't help me stop 'em."

"So you say. Just the same. You drop that gun and do it
now."

J.T. heard a commotion coming from the alley behind the
doctor's office as a pile of wooden crates were knocked over.
Toban and Jones were on the move. He knew he couldn't
afford to lose them again, but it was clear these two lawmen
weren't going to listen to him either. J.T. didn't like what
he was about to do, but they'd left him little choice. Lowering his gun to his side, he said, "Okay, boys, you win.
Here you go."

Twirling the gun butt around toward one of the deputies
he reached up as if he were going to hand him the weapon.
When the lawman leaned forward to take it, J.T. pushed the
lawman's gun to the side, struck him over the head with
barrel of the Peacemaker, then put a well-placed bullet into
the shoulder of the other, who yelled and dropped his gun
in the dirt as he was knocked out of his saddle.

Hurrying down the alley, J.T. found the doctor sitting on
the ground rubbing his head. A small trickle of blood made
its way down the side of his face. Kneeling down, J.T.
checked the wound. Jones had hit the man with his pistol.

"Which way did they go, Doc?"

"Cross the street, down that alley and to the left. I tried to
stop 'em but . . ."

J.T. raced across to the next alley. Out front people were
calling for a doctor for the wounded deputies. Reaching the
end of the alley, instinct caused J.T. to pull up short. They
could be waiting for him around the corner. Cocking the
hammer back on the Colt, he stepped out into the open then
quickly leaped back. The roar of two guns sounded in the
small confines of the alleyway as two bullets splintered the
wood at the corner of the building into a dozen pieces.

"Missed him, goddammit! Let's go."

J.T. heard the sound of boots running away and quickly

went around the corner in pursuit. He saw both men turn onto Main Street. Citizens were scrambling for cover as they saw the men with guns in their hands turn and fire back at the alley.

Inside the hotel restaurant, the first shots had sparked an interest as to what was happening outside. As more shots were fired, people began to leave their tables and walk out onto the boardwalk to see what was going on. Among them were Harrison, Lucy and Jack Corbin. The general suggested that it might not be safe for her on the street and that she should go back inside, but of course, she refused.

Suddenly the crowd saw two men coming down the street. One of them was staggering badly, but managed to fire two shots back toward an alleyway. The other man stopped and quickly began to reload his pistol. When Breed looked up again, he saw Corbin standing among the spectators in front of the hotel.

"What in the world is happening here?" said Harrison to no one in particular.

Corbin thought his heart was going to stop when he saw Breed and Toban standing in the middle of the street. Instinctively his hand went inside his coat for the short-barrel Colt he normally carried, but it wasn't there. He had seen no need to carry it to dinner and left it in his room.

Suddenly John Thomas Law was standing in the middle of the street facing Jones and Toban. Lucy cried out. "Oh, my God! That's John out there."

Corbin felt a knot forming in his gut. With any luck at all, the famed gunfighter would kill them both.

"Okay, boys! That's it. You're done. Now pitch then guns down. I don't want to have to kill you," said J.T.

Toban only laughed and continued to load his gun, while Choctaw, having finished that chore, now spun his a few times and dropped it down into his holster.

"You know we can't do that, Law," said Jones, as he stepped a few feet away from where Deke was squared off with J.T., and spread his feet slightly apart.

Deke, with his stitches torn apart and blood running down

the length of his pants leg, took a couple of steps to his right and holstered his gun.

"They say ya killed my little brother, John Law. That true?" asked Toban.

"Reckon it is, Deke. He didn't have the sand or the grit for a stand-up fight. Tried to gun Doc Holliday with a shotgun from ambush and that got him killed, sure enough."

"Ya didn't give him a chance, did ya?"

"Hell, no I didn't. He didn't deserve one. Just like you don't deserve one. But I'm givin' you that chance right now. You and Jones, both."

Deke's eyes went red as he yelled, "Ya go to hell, gunfighter!"

Toban's gun didn't make it past the top of his hoslter before J.T. put two .45 slugs in his chest. As the big man was falling, Choctaw Jones drew and fired once, his bullet burning a line across John Law's left cheek.

Law dropped to one knee and fired. His shot struck Breed in the right wrist, shattering the bone. His gun fell to the ground. But Breed was a hard man; he bent down to grab the gun with his left hand. J.T. fired again, breaking the left wrist. Jones cried out in pain as Law walked slowly toward him.

"Did Heck Ramsey cry out like that when you did the same to him, Breed? I doubt it. Now I'm going to ask you some questions. Who do you work for?"

Breed began to back up. He glanced toward Corbin, still standing in front of the hotel. It didn't go unnoticed by John Law, either.

"Who do you work for, Breed?"

Jones shook his head. He wouldn't answer. What was Law going to do, kill him?

He got his answer a second later as the Peacemaker roared again and a bullet shattered Breed's left kneecap. The man screamed and dropped to the ground.

J.T. was only fifteen feet away now. "Who do you work for, Breed? Who's the boss of your outfit? And don't tell me Toban."

Jones withered in the dirt, his blood slowly easing from his pain-wracked body.

"I don't know what you're talkin' about. Deke was my boss."

Law's .45 roared again, tearing a hole through Breed's right leg, just below the knee. The half-breed cried a pitiful cry, then began to weep openly from the pain.

Lucy Kincade stood watching in total horror as J.T. pulled the hammer back on his gun and again asked, "Give me a name, Breed—give me a name and it's finished."

Choctaw Jones was a shattered man. He knew Law wouldn't stop until he got what he wanted. Through eyes blurred by pain, Jones looked to Corbin for help, but the man wasn't about to make a move to expose himself and Jones knew it.

Lucy suddenly broke from the crowd and rushing up to J.T., screamed at him.

"Stop it! Stop it, John! My God—what kind of vile, sick degenerate could possibly do this to another human being. Stop it, I say!"

J.T. shoved her aside. He knew Breed was about to break. "Get away, Lucy."

Jones raised his head and cried out, "Goddammit, Corbin! Do something, you Yankee sonofabitch! You're supposed to be such a big man—do something, damn you!"

The crowd on the boardwalk let out a gasp and began to whisper among themselves as they moved away from Corbin. Harrison stared at Corbin in shocked disbelief and stepped back with the others. J.T. brought his gun up and started to turn away from Jones toward Corbin. Lucy mistakenly took the move to mean that J.T. was going to shoot Breed again. She reached out and grabbed his gun hand, pushing it aside as she screamed, "No! I won't let you do this!"

Corbin saw his chance. Leaping off the boardwalk, he dove into the dirt for Choctaw Jones's gun which lay only a feet from the hotel. Bringing the hammer back, he fired. The shot hit J.T. in the left forearm and passed clean through, but the impact spun him like a top, sending him and Lucy both into a heap in the middle of the street.

A second shot hit in the dirt inches from Law's head as he tried to push the girl clear of danger and at the same time shove her petticoats out of his face so he could see to shoot back.

"For godsakes, Lucy, get the hell out of the way!" he yelled.

Corbin was about to fire again when Lucy rolled away from J.T., giving him room to shoot. Both men fired at the same instant. J.T. saw the flash. He felt like his head was coming off; then everything faded to black.

When he finally came to, he found himself surrounded by people. He was in a bed. He knew that much. How he'd got there he had no idea. Among the onlookers were Harrison, Lucy, Jed Davis, the doctor and Cory Todd, the acting marshal. His arm hurt, but not nearly as bad as his head. The pain was terrible.

"Wha-what happened?" he asked.

The doc leaned in and checked the bandage around his head as he replied, "A fraction of an inch more to the right, son, and that bullet would have took your head clean off. You're a lucky man."

"You sure it didn't?' asked J.T.

Lucy knelt down next to him. "I'm sorry, John. I . . . I almost got you killed."

"But you didn't, that's all that matters. What about Corbin?"

Harrison stepped forward. "He's dead, John. You hit him right between the eyes. Hell, we all feel like fools. You're the only one who saw though the man. And there's a few other people besides Corbin who got things to answer for back at the capitol. So tell me, how'd you know he was Captain Jack?"

A slight smile broke at the corner of J.T.'s mouth. "I didn't know for sure. If Choctaw Jones hadn't broke when he did, I'd have been in a bad way tryin' to prove it, I suppose."

"Not really, Mister Law," said Cory Todd, stepping forward and holding Covington's telegram in his hand. "This here wire is from your Ranger friend down in Austin. They followed up on that information you sent them. Led straight to Corbin's spread. They found nearly five thousand head of stolen cattle and a chest full of money, gold coin, watches and such in the house. There was plenty of evidence in the safe, too. Lot of papers and stuff. Some of it must have been pretty important. They sent it straight to the governor's office. Jack Corbin was the leader of this outfit, no doubt about it."

Someone else was saying something, but the voice seemed to be fading away. John Law closed his eyes. He was so tired. The final words he heard as he drifted off to sleep were those of the doctor telling them all to leave.

ONE WEEK LATER, John Law rode out to the Circle H. His arm was still sore and he had a rather distracting part in his hair, but other than that he was feeling fine. The general and Jed Davis were glad to see him up and around. Josh was improving every day. He was sitting up now and eating just about everything in the house. He was surprised to find that Lucy had left to go back to Maryland. She had left a letter with the general to give to John T. when he came to visit. She had known he wouldn't leave Waco without looking in on Josh. He spent most of the day visiting with them all. Then after dinner, he told them it was time to go. Harrison told him he was welcome at his home any time he wanted to come. Josh thanked him for saving his life and Jed for helping to set the story straight about the past and ridding the county and the state of Corbin and his gang. All in all it had been one hell of an adventure. Waving a final goodbye, John Thomas Law headed out the gate and started south back toward Austin.

A few miles from the ranch, he paused and opened Lucy's letter. In it she again thanked him for Josh's life and apologized for almost getting him killed. She admitted to having feelings for him, but after seeing the dark side of him during the street fight, something had changed. Perhaps it was the sheer violence of it all. Or the look she saw in his eyes and on his face when he held a gun in his hand. Whatever it was, it was more than she could possibly deal with. They were from two different worlds; she knew that now. She would never forget him. She closed by saying that she hoped one day he would find whatever it was he wanted from life. But she feared that as long as he refused to set aside his gun, he was destined to travel alone in his world of violence, never knowing the peace she knew he wanted in his life. The last line read:

May God watch over you and keep you. Love, Lucy.

Pushing the letter down into his saddlebags, J.T. looked out across the rolling prairie that was Texas and wondered if there ever would be a time when a man wouldn't need a gun. Perhaps. Progress was already spreading across Texas. When it caught up with him—what would he do then?